THE ROYAL WAY

by André Malraux

André Malraux

THE
ROYAL
WAY

Translated by Stuart Gilbert

Published by Random House, New York

VINTAGE BOOKS
A DIVISION OF RANDOM HOUSE
New York

Part One

1

Now Claude's obsession mastered him again and he gazed fixedly at the man's shadowed face, straining to get at least some inkling of its expression, against the glow of a ship's lamp behind it. His features showed as vague as the dim radiance of the coastal lights on the Somali foreshore, lost in a blinding sheen of moonlight mirrored in the salterns. In his voice, too, there was an undertone of irony that seemed to lose itself in the dark immensity of Africa, mingling there with all the far-fetched legends his fellow-passengers, avid no less of gossip than of their day-long card-games, had woven round the man's strange personality—that fabulous aura of scandal, fantasy and fiction which always hovers about the

3

white man who has played a part in the affairs of independent Asiatic states.

"A man who's still young can make little or nothing of—what's the word for it?—of eroticism. Till he's turned forty he humbugs himself, he can't get 'love' out of his system. So long as he can't see a woman simply as a vehicle of sex, but takes her sexual function as a mere incidental adjunct of her womanhood, he's all for sentimental love—poor devil! But there's even worse in store: the time of life when the sex-obsessions of his boyhood start haunting him again, with all his memories to aggravate them."

Sniffing the dusty reek of flax and sheep's wool that still clung to his clothes, Claude saw once more the curtain of coarse sackcloth lifted from the doorway, and the arm pointing within to the girl's body he had watched a little while ago, poised there in its black nakedness, with a bright fleck of sunlight dappling the young, tip-tilted breast. How aptly, he mused, that droop of her thick eyelids expressed "eroticism," frenzied desire! "What that girl wants," Perken had then observed, "is to flay her senses to satiety."

"Memories!" Perken went on. "They're always taking new shapes. . . . What a queer thing imagination is! Like a foreign body lodged inside us, yet a part of ourselves for all that. Imagination—well, it makes up for everything!"

In the false light his sharp-cut profile hardly

showed at all; only between his lips there flashed an amber gleam, the gold tip of his cigarette, perhaps. Claude realized that his thoughts were moving on by slow degrees to join his words, like the skiff yonder gliding on towards them with a slow, rhythmic plash of oars, the ship's lights glinting on the oarsmen's swinging arms.

"What exactly do you mean?"

"Some day or other you'll find out for yourself. There's a great deal to be learned in a Somali brothel, as you'll discover."

Claude recognized the tone of bitter irony that a man seldom uses except when speaking of himself, or of his lot.

"Yes, much to learn," Perken repeated. Claude wondered what sort of lessons he might mean. He visualized the scene again: the yellow glow of oil-lamps ringed with insects, and the women, straight-nosed wenches with nothing of the negress about them except the dazzling white of their eyes, slotted between dark pupils and dusky cheeks. In time to a blind man's flute they paraded round and round in Indian file, each drumming furiously on the buttocks of the girl in front. Then abruptly, as the tune ended, they fell out of line and halted, prolonging with their voices the lascivious final note, their heads and shoulders motionless, their bodies tense with a deep excitement that found its only issue in the un-ceasing tremor of their arrowy breasts and supple loins, rippling with sweat under the lamplight. The brothel-keeper had pushed a smiling little girl towards Perken.

"No," he had said. "I want that one, over there. She, at least, doesn't look as if she enjoyed it."

Claude began to wonder—was the man a sadist? He had heard rumors of the missions on which Perken had been sent by the Siamese Government amongst the unpacified tribes of the interior, how he had organized the Shan tracts and the Lao frontier; he knew of the curious relations, sometimes cordial and sometimes acrimonious, between Perken and the Bangkok authorities, the mania he had displayed in earlier days for absolute power, a savage mastery of men, of which he would not brook the least control—and then of his decline, his "eroticism." Yet, on the voyage out, the women would have swarmed around him, had he given them a chance.

Yes, thought Claude, there's something queer about him; but it's hardly sadism.

Perken leaned his head against the back of the deck-chair, and now the light fell full on his features, the profile of a ruthless pro-consul, its brutality accentuated by shadows round the eyes and nostrils. The smoke of his cigarette rose straight into the air, merging into the velvet darkness.

The word "sadism," echoing in Claude's brain, called up a memory.

"One day in Paris I was taken to a small, shabby brothel. In the *salon* there was just one woman on view; she was strapped to an easel with her skirts turned up—it was like a scene from a Grand Guignol melodrama."

"With her face towards you, or her back?"

"Her back. Six or seven men were standing round; they looked like small tradesmen, with ready-made ties and alpaca coats. (It was summer, but nothing like so hot as this.) Their eyes were starting from their sockets and their faces scarlet, though they tried to act as if they'd come just out of curiosity. They went up to the woman one by one, and each in turn gave her a slap—only one apiece—then he paid up and filed out, or went upstairs."

"And that was all?"

"Absolutely. What's more, very few went upstairs; most of them just sloped off. I wonder what those chaps were thinking about as they put on their straw hats and straightened their coats!"

"Simple souls, I should say!"

Perken flung out his right arm as if to emphasize a remark, but the remark did not come forth. He seemed to hesitate, grappling with his thoughts.

"The great thing is—not to *know* the woman. She must stand for the opposite sex, no more than that."

"Not be an individual, you mean, with a life of her own?"

"And that's even truer for the masochists. It's with *themselves* they're fighting. A man ekes out his imagination as best he can, not as he chooses. Even the stupidest whore knows the gulf that lies between her and the man who tortures her, or whom she tortures.

7

Do you know the name they give abnormals? 'Thinkers,' they call them."

"Abnormals," Claude reflected; but wasn't that fellow, too . . . ? The man's face was working with emotion; Claude kept his eyes fixed on it. Was there a reason for the turn their conversation had taken?

"Yes," Perken resumed, " 'the thinkers.' It describes them very well. In fact there's only one 'sexual perversion,' as those fools call it, and it's when a man over-develops his imagination, and nothing in the world, no one, can wholly satisfy him. Out there, in Bangkok, I knew a man who used to have a woman tie him up, naked, for an hour or so in a dark room. . . ."

"And then?"

"That was all; he wanted no more than that. That fellow was the perfect, the consummate 'pervert.' "

He rose; was it to go to bed, Claude wondered, or to cut short the conversation? He watched Perken disappear behind a haze of smoke, picking his way across the prostrate forms of negroes asleep beside their coal-baskets with pink, wide-open mouths. His shadow dwindled and only that of Claude remained, splayed flat upon the deck. Seen thus in profile, his chin looked almost as obstinate, as masterful as Perken's stubborn jaw. Then the lamp swayed and the silhouette flickered. Two months hence how much of it would still remain, or of the body it prolonged? An eyeless form, lacking the resolute, yet unquiet, gaze that somehow expressed him so much better

8

to-night than yonder shadow at his feet, which the ship's cat was on the point of crossing. At a movement of his hand, the cat scurried away, and his obsession mastered him again.

Another fortnight to endure—long days of hope deferred, the craving of an addict balked of his drug. Fourteen more days at sea. He took out the archæological map of Siam and Cambodia once again; he knew it better than his own features. His eyes were fascinated by the thick blue rings with which he had encircled the Dead Cities, the dotted line that marked the ancient Royal Way, fraught with presentiments of a lingering end in the green depths of the Siamese forest. "It's an even chance I leave my bones there!" A maze of jungle tracks, strewn with the skeletons of small animals left to their fate beside the dying campfires, the tragic issue of the last expedition into the Jarai country—Odend'hal, the white chief, hammered to death with spear-hafts by the Sadete tribesmen, while close at hand the palm-fronds rustled in the darkness as the draught-elephants of the party forced their way through towards him. How many nights would he lie awake, pestered by mosquitoes, aching with exhaustion; or else asleep, dependent on his guide's precarious wakefulness? Seldom was there the chance of a fair fight. . . . Perken knew this part of the country well, but kept his peace about it. It was Perken's way of speaking that had first attracted Claude—he was the only passenger to pronounce such words as "nerve" and "enterprise" in a matter-of-fact tone—and it somehow conveyed to him how much he had in common with this ageing man whose hair was almost gray. Claude had heard his voice for the first time when they were steaming past a long red foreland of the Egyptian coast, and Perken was describing to an interested, if unfriendly, group of passengers how two skeletons (tomb-robbers, presumably) had been discovered during recent excavations in the Valley of the Kings; they were lying on the floor of an underground hall, flanked by galleries that were paneled, as far as eye could reach, with mummies of the sacred cats. Claude's experience of his fellow men was limited, but it had sufficed to convince him that as many fools are to be met with amongst adventurers as in other walks of life; Perken, however, definitely interested him. On a later occasion he heard him speak of Mayrena, and his brief kingship of the Sedangs.

"I see him as a player-king, bent on acting his own biography. You Frenchmen usually have a weakness for that sort of man, who prefers giving a fine performance to material success."

(Claude was reminded of his father who had joined up as a volunteer at the beginning of the war, and fell heroically on the Marne battlefield, only a few hours after writing to his son: *To-day, my dear boy, there's nothing they've not 'mobilized': civilization, justice, even the severed hands of little children. I've seen two or three displays of mass dementia in my time—the Dreyfus case was pretty successful in its way—but this one has the rest of them beaten all along the line, in kind as well as size.")*

"An attitude like his," Perken went on, "calls for displays of personal heroism, they're obviously in keeping with the rôle, and Mayrena played the hero right enough. He loaded the corpse of his young mistress, a Cham girl, on to his elephant and brought it back across a jungle teeming with hostile tribes, simply in order to bury her according to the customs of his race (the missionaries had refused her burial in their cemetery). You've probably heard how, to win the throne, he fought saber duels with a couple of Sedang chiefs, and held out for quite a while in the Jarai country—and that's not an easy thing to do."

"Do you know anyone who's stayed amongst the Jarais?"

"*I* did once; for exactly eight hours."

"Not very long!" Claude smiled.

Perken drew his left hand from his pocket and held it under Claude's eyes, spreading out the fingers; each of the three longest had a deep spiral groove gouged in it, corkscrew-wise.

"Drilled out; it took quite long enough."

Embarrassed by his indiscretion, Claude found nothing to say. Perken harked back to Mayrena.

"Anyhow he came to a bad end—like nearly everyone."

Claude had heard of the king's death-agony in a Malayan hut; how foiled ambition had gnawed at

11

his heart like a malignant tumor; how he had shuddered at the sound of his own voice reëchoed by the giant trees.

"Not so bad as all that."

"I don't approve of suicides."

"Why not?"

"Every suicide's egged on by a phantom self of his own making; when he kills himself he does it with an eye to—survival. Personally, I'd hate to let God make a fool of me."

Daily the affinity that Claude had surmised from the start was growing more apparent; the very tone of Perken's voice confirmed it, his way of saying "They" when he spoke of the other passengers (and, perhaps, mankind in general), as though by his indifference to claiming any social status he had set himself apart from them. The way he spoke suggested a wide, if somewhat warped, experience of humanity, and perfectly matched the expression of his eyes: a heavy, brooding look that suddenly grew hard as steel whenever some emphatic utterance set the slack muscles of his cheeks.

Now that Claude was almost alone on deck, he hesitated whether to read for a while, or give himself to thought—for sleep he could not. Or would he once again pore over the *Inventory,* and launch his imagination, like a man charging headfirst into a brick wall, against those citadels of dust, of green lianas and tall towers carved in the form of human faces that lay within the blue-ringed contours of the

Dead Cities, and, for all the dauntless faith that urged him on, encounter for the hundredth time the obstacles that cut across his dream, always at the same point, fatal and ineluctable?

Bab-el-Mandeb: the Gate of Death.

When they talked together Perken's allusions to a past of which Claude knew nothing always irritated him. The intimacy which had developed since their meeting at Djibouti (if Claude had entered that particular brothel it was because he had caught a glimpse of Perken's form within, under the outstretched arm of a gigantic negress swathed in black and red) had not allayed the urgent curiosity that drew him towards Perken; it was as if this man prefigured his own destiny. Moreover, the fighting spirit of one who, at the first onset of old age and isolation, deliberately cut himself adrift from human intercourse appealed to him. The elderly Armenian with whom Perken sometimes paced the deck, though obviously an old acquaintance, had little to say about him, and his reticence seemed deliberate, inspired, no doubt, by fear; he may have known Perken well, but he certainly was no friend of his. And, like the drone of the ship's engines persistent through the ebb and flow of conversations, Claude's feverish obsession with the jungle and the lost temples resumed its mastery, fixing his mood. It was as though the soul of Asia were making him her accomplice, flooding his mind with daydreams bred of old travelers'

13

tales and legendary lore: the marching forth of armies in the scented dusk loud with cicadas, the horses' hooves stirring up dust-clouds dark with slowly veering columns of mosquitoes, shrill cries of caravans beside the tepid fords, envoys waiting for the tide by mudflats spangled with shoals of stranded fishes, blued by a mist of butterflies above, and old kings rotten with caresses—and then that other dream, the dream that never left him, of shrines and gods of stone, mantled in green moss, frogs sprawling on their shoulders, their fallen heads beside them, pitted and time-scarred.

Perken had become a legendary figure on board, a constant theme of conversation for the passengers as they lounged in their deck-chairs; no less than the cantankerous boredom which develops on a long sea-voyage, or their anticipations, painful or otherwise, of journey's end, his personality had come to haunt their minds. But the "Perken myth" never took definite form; it was founded less on authenticated facts than on a puerile appetite for mystery, on loud stage-whispers uttered behind screening fingers. "Such a queer man, you know; simply ex-tra-ordinary!" All they could really know was that he had lived amongst the natives, ruled over them in districts where many of his predecessors had been killed, and it was rumored that the methods by which he had achieved this were more strenuous than law-abiding. Claude, however, judged that Perken's success was due more probably to his unflagging energy and certain soldierly qualities, combined with a remarkable broad-mindedness which enabled him to read the thoughts of beings widely different from himself—rather than to any buccaneering exploits. Never had Claude realized so clearly how these staid government officials, his fellow-passengers, hankered after romance, their hunger for the stuff of dreams, always at odds with their horror of being "humbugged" and of admitting the existence of a world so different from theirs. But, though these people swallowed wholesale the legend of Mayrena, who was dead—and that of Perken, too, perhaps, provided he were at a distance—here on board they were suspicious, up in arms against his silence, and resented his obvious determination to keep aloof from them, taking their vengeance in a supercilious attitude. Claude was alone in admiring Perken—perhaps, in understanding him—without attempting to pass judgment; all the same it had puzzled him at first that Perken put up with his company. He tried to understand him better, but found it hard to reconcile the romantic tales he heard—of messages conveyed in tubes stuck into corpses drifting down the river, during the settlement of the Shan Tracts; even of conjuring-tricks, and similar exploits—with what he judged to be the man's true character. For Perken, anyhow, would find no pleasure in "acting his own biography," nor would he need to admire his own achievements; rather, he was guided by some deep and steadfast purpose, vague hints of which Claude

15

sometimes caught, though he could not have put them into words. The captain, too, was conscious of it. "There's a streak of mysticism in every adventurer," he once said to Claude; but Perken's businesslike methods, his talent for organization, and his refusal to talk about his life greatly amazed him.

"He reminds me," the captain went on, "of one of those high officials of the Intelligence Service whom the British Government employs, and at the same time disowns. Still I don't see him ending his days in London as head of a department in the Street Service. For one thing, he's a German."

"A German? Isn't he a Dane?"

"Well, since the cession of Schleswig after the Treaty of Versailles, he's technically Danish. That suits his book; the cadres of the Siamese Police and Army are Danish. Really, of course, he's *heimatlos*. No, I don't think he'll wind up his career in an office; anyhow, as you see, he's coming back to Asia."

"In the service of the Siamese Government?"

"Yes and no—as usual! He's going to hunt for a fellow who has settled down—disappeared, more likely—in the unpacified area. But the really odd thing is that nowadays he's keen on making money; that's something new in him."

A curious bond had grown up between the younger and the older man. Whenever his obsession slowly lifted from his mind for the time being, leaving it open to other influences, Claude tried to analyse his feeling towards Perken. Perken was akin to

16

the only type of man with whom Claude's grandfather (who had brought him up) had felt the least
affinity. True, the resemblance was remote enough;
still they had the same dislike for all established
codes and the same taste for every form of human
activity, combined with an awareness of the futility
of action; but, above all, the same aversions. When
Claude tried to picture his own future, what he saw
there participated equally in his memories and in
Perken's personality; a two-fold, reiterated menace,
haunting as two parallel prognostications.

In his conversations with Perken all he could set
up against the other man's vast experience of life was
a fairly wide acquaintance with books; thus he had
been led to cite his grandfather much as Perken cited
real life, so as not to be perpetually countering actual
experiences with booklore, and to profit by the interest Perken showed in all adventurous careers. Moreover, whenever Perken talked of himself, the picture
of his grandfather always rose before Claude's eyes;
his white imperial, his loathing for the world in general, and his bitterness in speaking of his youth.
Proud of his pirate ancestors and their legendary
exploits, no less than of his stevedore grandfather,
delighted as any farmer patting his steers to pace the
decks of his own ships, he had devoted his youth to
building up the Vannec House, his passport to immortality.

He married when he was thirty-five; twelve days
after the wedding his wife returned to her parents.

Her father would have nothing to do with her; her mother, sagely disillusioned, counseled acquiescence. "Make the best of it, my dear child. All that, you know. . . . And, anyhow, when the children come . . ." And so forth. She went back to the old house he had bought for her, with a tall portico crowned with emblems of the sea and an immense courtyard hung with drying sails. She took down her parents' portraits and flung them under the bed, replacing them by a tiny crucifix. Her husband made no comment; for some days neither spoke a word. Then their married life resumed its even tenor. Inured to the tradition of hard work and loathing all romantic effusion, they gave no overt expression to the mutual dislike engendered by their early quarrel, but settled down to a tacit antipathy, much as chronic invalids learn to put up with illness. Both were equally tongue-tied where feelings were concerned, and it was in work that each of them sought to assert superiority over the other; work became their fetish, a drab but never-failing consolation. The coming of children brought a new element into their estrangement, making it all the more unbearable. With every balance-sheet their hatred flamed up again more furiously; long after sailors, deckhands, workmen, all had gone to bed and darkness fallen on the walls and the brown sails flapping in the courtyard, when the clocks chimed a late hour of the night, it often happened that one of them would lean out of a window, observe the lamp still burning in the other's room, and settle down to work again, though utterly worn out by the day's exertions. She was consumptive, but it made no difference to her; year after year he worked still later, so that his lamp should not be out before his wife's, which burnt on into the small hours of the night.

One day he noticed that the crucifix had gone to join the family portraits under the bed.

That he should suffer, not only by the loss of those he loved, but by the death of a woman he had never loved, struck him as preposterous; when his wife died, he took her loss with somber acquiescence. He had genuinely respected her, had known she was unhappy. Well, such was life. It was not so much her death as his own disgust with things in general that brought about the gradual decline of the Vannec House. When his fleet went down, almost to the last ship, off the Newfoundland coast, and the Insurance Company refused to compensate him; after he had spent a whole day dispensing little heaps of banknotes, equal in number to the lives lost, to his sailors' widows, he withdrew from active business, sick to death of money and money-making. Then came the years of endless litigation.

Innumerable, never-ending lawsuits. The dour old man gave vent to all the hatred of convention and propriety which so long had rankled in his heart. In the courtyard where the sails once flapped he lodged the traveling circuses which the municipality refused to harbor, and his old housekeeper opened wide the

19

gates through which no vehicle had passed for many a year, to let the elephant come in. Alone in the huge dining-room, seated in a richly sculptured chair, and sipping a glass of his finest wine, he slowly turned the pages of his ledger, evoking memories of the past.

In the old house the silence had grown deeper as, one by one, the children came of age and left it; not till Claude's arrival, in the course of the War, was the long silence broken. Now that his father was killed, his mother (who had left her husband some time before) came to see the child from time to time. She was alone in the world again, and old Vannec suggested she should come and live with him. So ingrained was his contempt for men and all their doings that he had come to regard them all alike with acrimonious indulgence. The idea that, while he still lived, his daughter-in-law should lodge in an hotel in his hometown displeased him, and he asked her to stay the night; only too well he knew that hospitality does not preclude dislike. They had conversed, or, rather, she had talked to him. She had lost all her friends, was growing old—her age oppressed her like a nightmare—and no hope of better days was left her; she looked on life with the indifference of despair. It would be possible, he thought, to live with her. If not quite penniless, she was badly off. Though he had little liking for the woman, yet a curious sense of comradeship drew him to her. She, like him, was cut off from human intercourse, from

all the absurd or calculated compromises it involves.
His cousin, an old woman now, was all but useless
as a housekeeper. He advised Claude's mother to stay
on, and she consented.

She rouged and powdered for her daylong solitude, for the portraits of dead owners of the house,
for the stone emblems of the sea—but, most of all to
reassure the woman she confronted in the mirror,
whose last resource lay in drawn curtains and a tactful twilight. Then, one day, she died prematurely at
the change of life; it seemed as if her dread of ageing had been founded on a premonition. He took
her death with grim approval. "At my age there's no
question of starting a new chapter." If this was fate's
last gesture in the tragi-comedy it had made of his
existence—well, he had nothing to say against it.
Henceforth he seldom departed from his rule of hostile silence, and unbent for Claude alone. With an
old man's subtle egoism he had almost always left
the task of punishing the child to the boy's mother,
or the tutor, or to his old cousin; thus he had always
impressed Claude, not only at Dunkirk, but later
too, when as a student in Paris, he made his uncles'
acquaintance, as possessing an exceptionally liberal,
far-ranging mind. For all his simplicity, the old man
had acquired a certain grandeur from his close asso-
ciation with death in many forms, and the tragic
glamour investing all who have passed a lifetime in
the service of the sea; there was much of an uncul-
tured Ecclesiast about him—but an Ecclesiast who

in no wise feared the Lord. Some of the phrases he coined to describe his vast experience of life resounded in Claude's ears like the low rumble of the closing hall-door penning them in at night against the outside world, the empty street. When, after dinner, his grandfather began to speak, and the tip of his pointed beard flickered against his chest, his slowly pondered words worked on Claude's imagination till he strove to fend them off, as if they came from an alien land far overseas, remote in time and space, whose denizens knew better than any men on earth the burden and the bitterness of life and the dark powers that govern it. "An old man's memory, Claude, is a damned family vault. More dead in it than living men. Don't I know them, our people! All of them—you, too—are cut in the same cloth. And when they try to break away . . . well, you've heard of crabs that nurse the parasites that prey on them, without the least idea of what they're doing. . . . Yes, Vannec blood always tells—for good or evil."

When Claude moved to Paris to continue his education, the old man formed a habit of going every day to the "Drowned Sailors' Wall"; he envied them their end, and found a solace for his own decline in the proximity of death. Then, one day, he had the idea of showing a young workman, who was dawdling at his job, how they used to hew ships' prows in his young days; a fit of dizziness came over him as he raised the two-edged axe, and it crashed into his skull.

In Perken's company Claude felt something of the attraction, compound of hostility and passionate devotion, inspired in him by the old man of seventy-six who had refused so valiantly to abdicate his past authority and died the death of an old Viking in his lonely house. What would be Perken's end? Once, gazing seawards, he had said to Claude: "I suspect that your grandfather was less significant than you imagine, and that you are considerably more so." It seemed that each of them expressed himself best indirectly, by parables; for it was under cover of their memories that they drew nearer to each other day by day.

Slashed by the rain, a dense mist swathed the ship. High above the line of lights that marked the docks, a flail of rays from the Colombo lighthouse raked the darkness. Gathered on deck, the passengers stared over the rain-drenched bulwarks towards the shimmering coast-line. The fat man standing beside Claude was helping an Armenian, a jewel-merchant visiting Ceylon to buy sapphires he would sell at Shanghai, to stack his trunks. In the offing Perken was talking to the captain; seen thus obliquely, his features looked less virile, above all when he smiled.

"I see you're squinting at old Chang's mug," observed the fat man. "Seen that way, he looks quite a good sort, don't he?"

"What's that you called him?"

"Oh, it's a name the Siamese have given him. The

23

elephant, it means; not the tame variety—the other sort, you know. It don't suit his build, but it's O.K. for his character, I guess."

The whiplash of the lighthouse beam swept round, dazzling them for a moment with its white intensity, then wheeled again into the darkness. Across a flurry of raindrops silvered by the decklights, they saw the gaunt outline of an anchored Arab sailing-ship, silhouetted from stem to stern against a gulf of darkness. When Perken moved a few steps forward, the fat man instinctively lowered his voice. Claude smiled.

"No, no! He doesn't scare me, not damned likely. I've done twenty-seven years out east. Not so dusty, eh? Still he's certainly a bit—er—awe-inspiring, well, you know what I mean. Don't you feel it, too?"

"It's all very fine and large," the Armenian remarked, but not over-loudly, "putting on airs like that; only it doesn't always come off. Not with us Parisians, anyhow."

"So you're a Parisian, eh?"

Getting his own back for some affront, Claude reflected. It looks as if he'd waited till he was just leaving the ship, before coming out with it. There had been no irony, but a good deal of bitterness in his voice.

Perken moved away again.

"Well, sir, I reckon myself a good Parisian. I was born in Constantinople, but I spend all the time I can in Paris. . . . No, as I said, it doesn't always pan out." He turned towards Claude. "You'll be through with him soon enough, my boy, like everybody else. He hasn't so much to boast of, anyhow. Now, if he'd had some technical knowledge—been a bit of an expert, so to speak—I can assure you, what with the power he had when he was running that bit of country for Siam, why he could have made a pile . . . a *pukka* fortune, damn it!"

He swung his arms windmill-wise in an emphatic circle, effacing for a moment the harbor lights that now shone nearer and more numerous, bathed in a watery glow, as if they too were porous, sodden with the downpour.

"Just think, man! There are Siamese bazaars only ten or fifteen days' march from the unpacified villages where you can still pick up rubies dirt cheap, provided you keep your wits about you and know how to trade with the natives. (Of course you're not in the business, so it doesn't mean much to you.) That would pay a damn sight better than bartering pinchbeck jewelry for those hand-made native trinkets of theirs—real gold, of course. Yes, even a youngster of twenty-three might have tumbled to that! What's more, it wasn't his own idea, really—a white man fixed it all up with the King of Siam fifty years ago—but he was set on visiting those parts. It's a wonder they didn't knock him on the head right away! He always wanted to act the boss. But, as I was just saying, a fellow can't always put it across as easy as that; and those folks in Europe made it pretty clear to him. Two hundred thousand francs! It's a damn sight harder to raise a big sum like that than to act the pocket-dictator. . . . Still, I ain't denying he's got the natives under his thumb all right."

"So he wants money, does he?"

"One thing's sure anyhow; he doesn't need it to live on, not up there."

Some launches had come alongside, laden with fruit and Indians who, as they clambered up the ladders, wrung out their dripping turbans. An hotel-tout captured the Armenian and led him away.

So he wants money, Claude repeated to himself.

"Old monkey-face wasn't far wrong about that," the fat man observed. "You can live on next to nothing in those parts."

"You're in the Forest Service?"

"Yes. Head Ranger."

Claude felt his fixed idea possessing him again, insistent as a fever in his blood; this man's knowledge of the country might be of service for the desperate venture on which he was embarking.

"Ever used buffalo-carts on your travels up-country?"

"That's a good one! Why, of course."

"What load can they really take?"

"Well, they're small you know; it all depends on the weight of your stuff. . . ."

"Stones, for instance?"

"Well, the 'regulation load' as they call it is a hundred and twenty pounds."

Like so many official regulations in the Colonies, Claude reflected, the "regulation load" might be merely so much eyewash. Otherwise he'd have to give up the idea of using buffalo-carts. . . . So even here it dogged him—that specter of defeat and death out in the jungle. Any idea of using coolie transport for blocks of stone weighing four hundred pounds or more must obviously be ruled out. What about elephants, then?

"Elephants, my boy, I can tell you all about 'em; it's only a matter of knowing the ropes. People say the elephant's a delicate beast. Not a bit of it! An elephant's not in the least delicate. The trouble is, the animal can't abide shafts or traces; they gall him. Well then, how do you get round it? What?"

"I'm listening."

"You take an auto tire, any old Michelin will do, and slip it over the elephant's neck, like a napkin-ring. See? Then you hook your stuff on to the tire. That's all there is to it. The rubber's soft on the brute's neck, you see."

"Can one get elephants up-country, north of Angkor?"

"Far north?"

"Yes."

There was a moment's silence.

"Beyond the Dang-Reks, you mean?"

"Up to the Se-Mun."

"A white man who tries to explore that region by himself hasn't a dog's chance."

27

"Can one get elephants there?"

"Well, it's your picnic, young man, not mine. . . . Elephants? Well, I'd be surprised if you got 'em; the natives don't relish the idea of traveling in those parts, you see. You're quite likely to run across the wild Mois—and that's no laughing matter, let me tell you. Then the folk in those villages at the back of beyond are rotten with malaria, why their eyelids are all blue, like someone'd been bashing 'em for a week on end! So, of course, there's no getting any work out of that lot. Then, happen you're stung—as you're damned sure to be—you can bet your boots it's one of the damned fever-carrying mosquitoes has done it. And then, too, there's . . . but that'll do for to-day, I should think. Coming on shore for a stroll? Here's the launch."

"No."

He harked back to his musings. If he's out for money, it's not because he needs it for himself—not up there, anyhow. Then what can he need it for, I wonder . . . More potent than the menace of the jungle that "Perken legend," ill-natured doubtless, yet somehow grandiose, was working on Claude like a ferment, like the darkness all around him, disintegrating all that he had deemed the real world. On one of the ships in harbor a siren hooted, calling for dinghies to come up alongside, and as the long-drawn, urgent call failed on the sodden air, the city seemed to grow remoter still, to melt away into the shadows of the Indian night. In this phantom world, unstable as mirage, his last thoughts of the West fell from him; wave on wave, serenely, a cool wind lapped his temples, and under its soft insistence he saw Perken with new eyes—no longer as a man apart, but as one in harmony with all around him. Like all who pit themselves against the world, Claude was drawn to men of his own stamp and eager to read greatness into them; in such cases he cared little if he duped himself. If Perken wanted money it was not to indulge some such harmless hobby as collecting tulips. And yet, persistent as the muted hum of distant crickets droning through the silence, that topic, money, had always hovered in the background, whenever Perken described his past experiences. The Captain, too, had noticed it. "Nowadays he's keen on making money."

What had the Forest Ranger said? "A white man who tries to explore that region by himself hasn't a dog's chance."

Not a dog's chance . . . !

Well . . . at this hour Perken was to be found, most likely, at the bar.

2

Claude had no difficulty in finding Perken. He was seated at one of the wicker tables which the stewards had brought out on deck. In one hand he held the stem of a wine-glass that stood on the table-cloth, but his back was turned and his other hand rested on the bulwark; he was watching, it seemed, the lights that flickered still far away down the harbor.

Claude felt ill at ease, like an intruder.

"Well, there's my last port of call." Perken pointed towards the lights. It was his left hand he lifted; lit up by the deck-lamps, it stood out for a moment darkly silhouetted against a sky washed clean of clouds and bright with stars. The grooves gouged in the fingers showed as sinuous black streaks. Then he swung round towards Claude, who caught a look of deep dejection on his face; the injured hand dropped out of sight.

"We're sailing in an hour. . . . By the way, what will the journey's end mean—for you?"

"Doing things instead of dreaming them. And, for you, what . . . ?"

Perken's gesture seemed to wave aside the question. Still he answered: "Wasting time."

Claude threw him a questioning glance; he closed his eyes. "A bad start," the young man thought; "better try something else."

"Will you be going amongst the unpacified tribes?"

"I shouldn't call that 'wasting time'; quite the contrary."

Once more Claude felt at a loss. At a venture he repeated Perken's words.

"The contrary?"

"I've found out pretty nearly everything that's to be found up there."

"Everything except money, you mean?"

Perken eyed him shrewdly, but did not answer.

"But supposing," Claude persisted, "it was to be found 'up there'?"

"Well, just you try to find it!"

"I might. . . ." Claude hesitated for a moment; from a temple on shore there came a drone of chanting voices, punctuated now and then by the brief stridence of a motor-horn. "In the jungle between the Laos and the sea," he continued, "there are quite a

31

number of temples Europeans know nothing about."

"With idols in solid gold, and so forth? I've heard that tale before!"

"Bas-reliefs and statues—not in gold at all—are worth quite a lot of money." Again Claude hesitated before continuing. "You'd like to see your way to a couple of hundred thousand francs, I believe?"

"So the Armenian's been blabbing, has he? Well, I make no mystery of it anyhow. . . . Why not have a shot at the Egyptian tombs, while you're about it?"

"Do you really see me digging for the Pharaohs and their precious cats?"

Perken seemed lost in thought. Watching him, Claude realized that a past record, the facts of a career, are quite as impotent in certain cases to damage a man's prestige as to mar a woman's charm. At this moment the tales of bartered trinkets, Perken's early history, simply did not exist; so *real* was he, standing there, that the things he had done fell from him, like idle dreams. Of the "facts" of Perken's life Claude would accept none but those which tallied with his vision of the man. Would he reply? Claude wondered.

"What about a stroll?"

They took some steps in silence. Perken still had his eyes fixed on the yellow harbor-lights which now shone steadily beneath a sky of brighter stars. Though night had come the air was clammy as ever; whenever Claude ceased speaking he was conscious of it clinging to his skin, like a moist perspiring hand. He drew a cigarette from a packet, then, vexed by the trivial gesture, flung it overboard.

"I've come across some temples," Perken said after a while. "But, for one thing, they haven't all got carvings. . . ."

"No. But many have."

"Cassirer of Berlin paid five thousand marks for the two Buddhas Damrong gave me. But, as for looking for old sculpture—why, you might as well go treasure-hunting, like the natives."

"Supposing you knew for certain that fifty treasure-hoards had been cached on a river bank between two given points—six hundred yards apart, let's say— would you look for them?"

"There's no such river."

"Perhaps not. . . . Will you try to find the treasure?"

"For you?"

"Sharing with me; fifty, fifty."

"And your river . . . ?"

Perken's faint smile exasperated Claude.

"Come and see."

In the corridor leading to Claude's cabin Perken placed his hand on the young man's shoulder.

"You gave me to understand yesterday that you were playing your last card. Is what you've just been telling me concerned with that?"

"Yes."

Claude had expected to find the map spread out on his bunk, but the cabin-steward had folded it up. He opened it.

"Those are the lakes. The red spots clustering round them are the lake temples; the other red spots you see dotted about the map are other temples."

"And the blue patches?"

"The dead cities of Cambodia. All have been explored already. I think there are more of them—but that's another story. This is my point; d'you notice that the red dots—the temples, that is—are thickest where that black line begins, and, what's more, that they tend to run parallel with it?"

"What's your black line?"

"The Royal Way, the road that linked up Angkor and the lakes with the Menam river basin. It was quite as important in its day as the road between the Rhone and the Rhine was in the Middle Ages."

"Let's see. The temples follow the road as far as . . . ?"

"Up to the limit of the *really* explored area. (The exact name of the place doesn't matter.) My theory is that if you follow, by compass, the line of the old road, you're bound to come on temples. Supposing Europe became covered with a dense forest, wouldn't it be absurd to imagine you could travel from Marseilles to Cologne by way of the Rhone and the Rhine, without coming across ruined churches? And don't forget that, as far as the explored area is concerned, the truth of my theory can be tested; has, in fact, been verified. All the old travelers' tales confirm it."

He broke off, to answer Perken's enquiring gaze.

"No," he continued, "I haven't fallen from the clouds—merely from the College of Oriental Studies; and Sanskrit has its uses. . . . What's more, all the officials who have ventured into those parts, a few dozen miles or so beyond the charted area, bear me out."

"Do you suppose you're the first to have deduced this from the map?"

"The Land Survey Department doesn't bother much about archæology."

"But what about the French Institute?"

Claude opened the "Inventory" at a marked page; some passages had been underlined. *"The monuments lying outside our itineraries remain to be collated. . . . We are far from claiming that the lists we have compiled are exhaustive."*

"That," Claude said, "is the report of the last great archæological survey of the country."

Perken glanced at the date. "1908?"

"Between 1908 and the War," Claude replied, "nothing much was done. And, after that, only local explorations were made. Any way it's all rough-and-ready work. I've cross-checked the distances and discovered that their estimates of the metric units employed by early explorers need overhauling, and several statements—very encouraging ones, too—

35

which they dismiss as mere folk-tales should be verified along the Royal Way itself. And we're only speaking of Cambodia, mind you; as you know, next to nothing's been done in Siam."

He paused, expecting an answer or a comment, but none was forthcoming. "What are you thinking about?" he asked at last.

"Well, the compass would give a rough indication, of course; and I suppose you're counting on the natives for further information?"

"Yes; on those, of course, whose villages aren't too far from the Royal Way."

"Perhaps. . . . In Siam, anyhow, I know the language well enough to get them to talk. I've seen some of those temples myself; the old Brahminic temples you mean, don't you?"

"Yes."

"Then we shouldn't come up against fanatics, we'd have Buddhists to deal with all the time. Yes, perhaps it isn't such a wildcat scheme, after all. Know much about their art?"

"I've been studying nothing else for quite a while."

"Quite a while, eh? By the way, what's your age?"

"Twenty-six."

"Twenty-six!"

"Well, I know I look younger. . . ."

"It wasn't astonishment," Perken explained; "merely—envy." There was no irony in his voice.

36

"The French Administration, you know, hasn't much liking for . . ."

"I've been sent here on a mission."

Perken was dumbfounded for a moment.

"Ah, now I'm beginning to see daylight," he remarked.

"Oh, unpaid, of course. Our ministries are obliging enough when it costs them nothing."

A picture rose before his eyes of the high functionary, affable and pompous, who had interviewed him; the endless, empty corridors; the sunlight falling on ingenuous maps where far-flung cities, Djibouti, Vinh-Tian and Timbuctoo, stood out like capitals in vast pink patches, the red and gilded furniture, blatant as a sumptuous stage setting.

"I see," Perken said. "Friendly relations with the Hanoi authorities, and permits to levy transport; *I* see. . . . Not very much, still it's something." His eyes fell on the map again. "For transport—buffalo-carts, of course."

"By the way, how's one to take the official limit, a hundred and twenty pounds?"

"A dead letter. Anything from a hundred to six hundred pounds; depends on what . . . on what you come across. Carts, then. If, after a month's exploring, there's nothing doing . . ."

"No likelihood of that. You know, of course, that the Dang-Rek country is quite unexplored."

"Less than you think."

"And the natives know about the temples. What do you mean by 'less than you think'?"

"We'll come back to that." He was silent for a while. "I know the ways of the French Administration. You don't belong to it, and they'll put every obstacle in your path. Still that's not the real danger. No, there's a more serious one, even if there are two of us."

"Meaning?"

"The danger of leaving our bones there."

"The Mois, you mean?"

"The Mois, the jungle, malaria."

"I'd guessed as much."

"Then we'll let the subject drop. Personally, I'm used to it. Let's talk money instead."

"Simple enough! A small bas-relief, almost any statue, will fetch thirty thousand francs or so."

"Gold francs?"

"That's asking too much, I'm afraid."

"A pity! Then I'll want ten at least, and ten more for you; twenty, all told."

"Twenty sculptures."

"A tall order—but feasible, I think."

"And don't forget that a single bas-relief, if it's first-class, a dancing-girl for instance, sells for a couple of hundred thousand francs at least."

"How many stones would go to make it?"

"Three or four."

"And you're sure of selling them?"

"Dead sure. I know the biggest dealers in London and Paris. And it's easy to fix up a public sale."

"Easy perhaps, but a longish job, eh?"

"There's nothing to prevent your selling directly —without a public auction, I mean. Pieces of that sort are extremely rare; the boom in far-eastern curios started at the end of the war, and there've been no new finds."

"There's another point; suppose we find the temples"—"*We*," Claude murmured to himself—"how do you propose to dismantle the stones?"

"That's the problem. I thought of . . ."

"They're big blocks, if I remember rightly."

"Yes; but don't forget that the Khmer temples were built without foundations or cement. Like castles made of dominoes."

"And each of your dominoes is—wait a bit!—a good yard long by eighteen inches deep and wide. Fifteen hundred pounds or so. Nice little things to handle!"

"I'd thought of using rip-saws and removing only the carved surface, just a thin slab. Nothing doing. Hack-saws will be quicker; I've brought some with me. And then we can reckon on the work of time; it has dismantled them pretty effectively; so have the peepuls sprouting in the crannies, not to mention the Siamese fire-raisers who took a hand at the good work, and did it thoroughly."

"I've come across more mounds of broken débris

than temples. Don't forget the treasure-hunters, too, have been that way. Till now I've looked on the temples from that angle, myself, more or less."

Perken had put down the map and was staring up at the electric bulb. Claude wondered what his musings were; for his eyes seemed focused on some distant vision, a dreamer's eyes. "What do I really know of the man?" he asked himself again, struck by the profile harshly outlined against the washstand. The slow, deep thudding of the engines pounded on the silence, as though to break down his opposition, force his acquiescence.

"Well then?"

Perken pushed aside the map and sat down on the bunk.

"Let's cut out possible objections. When all's said and done, your plan is sound enough. No, I wasn't thinking it over; I was dreaming of the time when I'd have the money in my hands. Anyhow it's not my way to tackle enterprises which are all plain sailing; that's the sort I always botch. Still, you'd better know that, if I come in with you, it's because I'm due to go into the Moi country in any case."

"What part of it?"

"Further north; but that's no obstacle. I shan't know exactly what my destination is till I reach Bangkok. I'm going to try to find—to track down—a man for whom I once had much regard, and a good deal of mistrust. When I reach Bangkok I'll be given the latest reports that have come in from the district

40

about his disappearance (as they call it). I believe . . ."

"Then you come in with me?"

"Yes. I believe he set out for the part of the country in which I'm interested. If he's dead things will
be easy enough. Otherwise . . ."

"Yes?"

"I don't want him about. He'd spoil everything."

The transition from one subject to the other had
been so abrupt that Claude could hardly bring himself to listen. Once his acceptance given, the man
himself had almost ceased to count. Claude followed
Perken's gaze; it was riveted on Claude's reflection
in the glass. For an instant he, too, scanned through
alien eyes his forehead and projecting chin. And, like
his eyes, his companion's thoughts were doubtless
fixed on him.

"Don't answer me unless you want to."

Perken's gaze grew more intent.

"What's the idea behind this expedition?"

"I might reply—it would be the truth—that I
have hardly any money left."

"There are other ways of making it. And what do
you want money for? As far as I can judge, it's not
just for buying 'a good time.' "

"What about *you?*" Claude all but asked aloud.
Then he said: "A man who's poor can't choose his
enemies. I mistrust the small change of revolt. . . ."

Perken was still watching Claude with a curious
look, searching and far away at once, and fraught

41

'with memories; it reminded Claude of the gaze of an intelligent priest. Then his eyes hardened.

"No man ever makes anything of his life."

"But life makes something of us."

"Not always. What do you expect from yours?"

Claude did not reply at once. His companion's career had been so perfectly metabolized into experience, into half-formulated thoughts, into his gaze, that the crude facts of his life, his "biography," had ceased to matter. All that now held the two of them together, the source of their fraternity, was what lies deepest in the heart of man.

"What I know best is what I do *not* expect of it."

"Whenever you've had to choose between alternatives, surely . . ."

"It's not I who choose; it's something in me that resists."

"Resists what?"

He had put the question to himself often enough to be able to give a prompt reply.

"The idea of death."

"Death, the real death, is a man's gradual decline." Perken's eyes had strayed to his reflected self. "Yes, growing old is infinitely worse. Having to accept one's destiny, one's place in the world; to feel shut up in a life there's no escaping, like a dog in its kennel! A young man can never know what death really is."

Suddenly Claude realized what the link between them was, between him and this man who had accepted his companionship—why he hardly knew: their common obsession with death.

Perken picked up the map.

"I'll bring it back to-morrow."

Like a cell door the atmosphere of the cabin closed in on Claude once more, and, like a fellow-prisoner, Perken's question kept him company. Their disagreement, too. No, there were not so many avenues to freedom, after all. Though he was not simpleton enough to be surprised by them, he had, in earlier days, reflected on the conditions of a civilization which gives such a place to intellect that those who make of it their staple fare, surfeited presumably by its excess, are, gently but firmly, piloted towards the bread-line. What career to choose, then? He had no wish to deal in motor-cars or bonds or eloquence like some of his friends, whose well-oiled hair announced their social luster; nor to build bridges like those other friends whose ill-kempt locks vouched for their technical abilities. What did they work for, those friends of his, except to cut a figure, to be looked up to? That was their aim, and, for himself, he loathed it. For the childless, godless modern man such truckling to the established order impressed him as an abject surrender to the power of death. So he must forge for himself weapons other than the weapons of the herd; and the surest arm for one who feels himself cut off from his kind is courage.

All the outworn ideas of those who deemed their

lives mere stepping-stones towards a nebulous "salvation" were dead ideas—and what had he to do with corpses? Corpse-like, too, the homilies of those who would adjust their lives to a set pattern. For other men that rankling preoccupation with the unknown might spell a blind surrender to the buffetings of chance, but he had come to treat the lack of finality inherent in all life as an incentive, rather, to activity. Ah, how he longed to wrench his dreams clear of the inert world that shackled them!

"Adventure, as they call it," he reflected, "isn't an evasion, but a quest. A break in the established order is never the work of chance; it is the outcome of a man's resolve to turn life to account." He knew the type of man for whom adventure is the food of dreams—a childish game of make-believe—and he knew, too, that adventure often serves to keep the secret fire of hope aglow. Futilities! The fixed idea which he had spoken of to Perken, the sense of death's austere dominion, pervaded all his being, persistent as the throb of blood across his temples, imperious as sexual desire. He might be killed, might disappear—it mattered little to him, for he had small interest in his own survival—yet, thus at least, he would have had the fight, if not the victory. But, living, to endure the vanity of life gnawing him like a cancer; all his life long to feel the sweat of death lie clammy on his palm . . . unbearable! Whence, indeed, if not from death, came his fierce desire, dense with the odor of death-ridden flesh, for all that is immortal? What was his quest of the unknown, the slave's brief spell of freedom from his master, that men who do not understand it call adventure—what was it but his counterattack on death? So, like a blind man wildly lashing out, he strove to fight death down—and make a sport of it. . . .

Could he but break away from the drab and dusty life of those around him, and at last attain something beyond, something outside himself . . . !

Perken had landed at Singapore and was to proceed directly to Bangkok. Everything had been arranged between them. Claude was to rejoin him at Pnom-Penh after having his explorer's brevet visaed at Saigon and calling at the French Institute. The first steps to be taken would depend on the terms he came to with the Director of an Institute which looked on ventures such as his without amenity.

One morning—stormy weather had set in again—looking through his cabin port-hole, he noticed some of the passengers pointing to an object out at sea. He ran up on deck. Through an opening in the cloud-bank a wan and watery ray of sunlight fell on the low Sumatra coastline, level with the tumbling waves. Through his field-glasses he could see the dense green tangle of the forest billowing down towards the foreshore, topped here and there by palm-trees, black against the gray expanse of sea and sky. Here and there on the high summits pale fires flickered, capped with heavy plumes of smoke; on the

45

lower slopes the tree-ferns stood out clearly against dark gulfs of shadow. He could not take his eyes off the dark abysses that seemed to swallow up the foliage. Could a man possibly force his way through that serried undergrowth? Well, if others had contrived to do it, so could he. Against his dubious affirmation the lowering sky and the impenetrable tangle of the leafage, teeming with insect-life, affirmed their silent menace.

He went back to the cabin. So long as he had brooded over it in solitude, his plan had cut him off from the world, and penned him in a private universe as incommunicable as the blind man's or the lunatic's, a universe in which, whenever his attention flagged, the forest and its temples seemed gradually to come to monstrous life, malevolent as the great beasts of the jungle. Perken's presence had brought things back to the human, normal plane; yet now again he let himself relapse, with full awareness, into the dream-world of hallucination. Once again he opened his books at the marked pages. *"The decorative motifs have greatly suffered from the constant humidity of the undergrowth and the violence of the tropical rainfall. . . . The vault has caved in completely. . . . It is certain that further discoveries are to be made in this region, which nowadays is practically uninhabited and overgrown with scrub jungle where herds of elephants and wild buffaloes roam. . . . The blocks of sandstone of which the arches were constructed litter the interior of the cloisters in*

an inextricable confusion; the highly regrettable
state of dilapidation which prevails seems due to the
use of wood as a building material. . . . Here and
there large trees have sprouted in the débris and
grown so tall as to overtop the coping of the walls;
their gnarled and knotted roots have tightened
round the stones and welded them together. . . .
The whole region is practically a desert." What
would be his weapons in the fight that lay before
him? At each *crescendo* of the clanging engines he repeated over and over again, as if to exorcise a phantom from his mind: French Institute, French Institute, French Institute! "I know that crowd," Perken
had told him; "you don't belong there." A pointer.
Well, he'd be on his guard. And, in any case, he
knew how quick men are to discern such as reject
their social compromises; that an atheist causes far
more scandal now that faith has passed away. Truths
that his grandfather had dinned into his ears time
and time again. . . . And to think that the best part
of his weapons were in those fellows' hands! . . .

Ah, could he but shake off the wearisome inertia
of the voyage, the tyranny of dreams and hopes deferred!

3

Stroking his light brown beard, Albert Ramèges, Director of the French Institute, watched M. Vannec enter. He was seated at his desk, facing the window, a rectangle of light framing a clump of palm-trees and a wall stained blue-green by the tropical rains.

"The Colonial Office, Monsieur Vannec, informed me of your departure, and I was pleased to receive your telephone message yesterday and learn that you had arrived. Needless to say, we shall do everything in our power to assist you. You will find our staff friendliness itself and they'll be delighted to furnish any advice you may require. Well, we'll go into details about that presently."

He rose from his chair and sat down beside

48

Claude. Here begins the "friendliness," Claude said to himself. The director's voice became still more affable.

"I am very pleased to make your acquaintance, my dear Monsieur Vannec. I read the interesting essays on Asiatic art which you published last year, with the greatest attention. And, since hearing you had landed, I've been looking into your theory. I must own that I was more interested than convinced by the arguments that you set forth; yes, I was definitely interested. Your generation has an odd way of looking at things."

"I stated those theories with a view to—" "clearing the ground," he almost said, but thought better of it—"with a view to being free to advance towards another idea, which interests me more. . . ."

Ramèges cast him a questioning look. Claude was keenly aware of his desire to prove himself detached, aloof from his official functions, not to say above them, and to treat him like a guest. Out of boredom, perhaps, or was it some vague loyalty towards his own clan? Claude knew of the ridiculous feud persisting between all other archæologists and those whose knowledge derives from philological research. Ramèges' mind was obviously full of the Institute; Claude dared not broach the question of his mission right away—his interlocutor would have taken it almost as an affront.

"My view is," Claude continued, "that the personal value we set on an artist may blind us to one of the main factors determining the vitality of his work. I refer to the cultural status of the successive generations appraising it. It looks as if, in matters of art, the time-factor were deliberately ignored. What interests me personally, I must say, is the slow disintegration, the gradual change that comes over such works—their secret life which battens on men's deaths. Every work of art, in fact, tends to develop into a myth."

He realized that he had expressed himself too tersely, that he might seem obscure; he was handicapped by his eagerness to get down to the object of his visit, and at the same time to humor the Director, whose curiosity was certainly aroused. Ramèges was in a brown study. The splash of heavy raindrops falling one by one outside the window echoed in the room.

"In any case, it's a curious idea. . . ."

"For me museums are places where the works of an earlier epoch which have developed into myths lie sleeping—surviving on the historical plane alone —waiting for the day to come when artists will wake them to an active existence. If they have a definite appeal for me it is because I know the artist has this power of summoning them back to a new lease of life. In the last analysis, of course, no civilization is ever understood by another one. But its creations remain—only we are blind to them until our myths come into line with theirs."

Attentive now and curious, Ramèges went on smiling. He takes me for a theory-monger, Claude thought. Sallow, he looks; abscess of the liver, most likely. He'd understand me far better if he could realize that what draws me to all these things is the obstinate desire that every artist has to ward off death by a sort of intermittent immortality—if, in fact, I linked up what I've just been saying with his abscess. Better change the subject! . . . Claude, too, began to smile and Ramèges took the smile to mean the young man wanted to make himself agreeable; the atmosphere grew more cordial.

"The truth is," the Director summed it up, "you're not sure of yourself. Oh, I know it's not always an easy matter to keep one's self-confidence. Do you see that scrap of pottery—yes, that's it—under the book? It was sent us from Tientsin. The designs are undoubtedly Greek, archaic Greek, of the sixth century B.C. at the latest. And look what's on the shield—a Chinese dragon! Yes, we've got to overhaul our views about the relations between Europe and Asia before the Christian Era pretty thoroughly. There's no escaping it. When competent authority proves we've gone astray there's nothing for it but to make a fresh start."

The sadness with which Ramèges spoke made Claude feel more in sympathy with him. Had those discoveries compelled him to abandon some task on which he had expended much time and labor? To avoid his eyes, Claude began examining a pile of photographs, divided into two series, of Khmer and

Cham statuary respectively. To break the silence which had grown up between them, Claude asked: "Which do you prefer?" He pointed to the two sets of pictures.

"How should I have any preference? Archæology's my line."

His tone implied that he had left behind such naïve preoccupations, the toys of youth. He felt he had lost ground and was vaguely irritated. Questioning apart, he meant to keep the upper hand in the interview.

"Let's hear about your projects, Monsieur Vannec. You intend, if I'm not mistaken, to explore the regions lying along the line of the ancient Royal Road of the Khmers?"

Claude nodded.

"I may as well tell you at once that the track—not to mention the road itself—is quite obliterated over long stretches, and near the Dang-Rek range disappears completely."

"I'll find it," Claude smiled.

"Well, let's hope so—for your sake! It is my duty, my official duty, to warn you of the danger you will incur. You are doubtless aware that two of the leaders of official exploring parties, Henri Maître and Odend'hal, were murdered there. And yet our unfortunate countrymen knew that part of the country very well."

"It will come as no surprise to you, I imagine, if I tell you that I'm not looking forward to an easy time—or a quiet life. . . . But may I ask you, sir, what facilities you will put at my disposal?"

"You'll be given supply warrants which will enable you—on application to the local Deputy Resident, needless to say—to procure native carts and cartmen for the transport of your kit. Fortunately, an expedition like yours travels comparatively light."

"Do you call stones light objects?"

"It has been decided—to prevent any repetition of the regrettable incidents of last year—that all objects of whatever nature shall be left *in situ.*"

"I beg your pardon?"

"*In situ*—where they are. A report will be drawn up about them. After perusing it, the Head of our Archæological Department will, if necessary, proceed . . ."

"From what you've told me, it doesn't seem likely that the Head of your Archæological Department will venture into the regions I propose to explore."

"Well, it's a special case. We shall look into it."

"And, what's more, supposing he's willing to risk his neck there, I'd like to know why I should go pioneering just for his benefit."

"You'd rather do it for your own, eh?" Ramèges mildly suggested.

"In the last twenty years your official parties haven't once touched that region. No doubt they'd better things to do. Personally, I know the risks involved—and I want to run them without official control."

"But not without official assistance, I think?"

Both men were speaking coolly, without raising their voices. Claude was fighting down the blind fury that was rising in him. . . . What right had this official to claim a title over any objects he, Claude, might discover, to hunt for which he had come here, on which his last hope hung?

"With only the assistance that has been promised me. With less assistance than you would give a Survey Officer crossing one of the administered areas."

"You hardly expect Government to give you a military escort, I presume?"

"Have I asked for anything more than what you offered me yourself, the right to requisition cartmen —the least you can do, in fact?"

Ramèges gazed at him without speaking. After a moment's desultory silence, Claude caught himself listening for the sound of raindrops outside; they had ceased falling.

"There are only two alternatives," he went on presently. "Either I never return, and that's an end of it; or I return and whatever profit I may personally make will be a trifle beside the *data* I shall bring back."

"For whose benefit—your *data?*"

"I won't do you the injustice, sir, of believing you turn down as a matter of course any and every contribution to art-history that doesn't come from the Institute over which you preside."

"Unfortunately the value of such contributions is

only too dependent on the technical training and experience—not to mention the sense of discipline—possessed by those who make them."

"It's not his sense of discipline that usually takes a man to the unpacified tracts!"

"I agree. But what takes a man there may be . . ."

Leaving his remark unfinished, Ramèges rose from his seat.

"Anyhow, Monsieur Vannec, I am to give you my assistance, within certain limits. You may count on me for that. As for the rest . . ."

"For the rest . . ." Claude's gesture indicated, as tactfully as might be, "I'll see to it myself."

"When will you be starting?"

"As soon as possible."

"You shall have the papers to-morrow afternoon."

The Director showed Claude out with the utmost courtesy.

"Well, what about it?" he asked himself as he crossed the compound; then, as though to postpone further reflection, he fell to gazing at the shattered gods of stone on which belated lizards flickered to and fro.

"Let's figure things out!"

It was beyond him. He entered the empty boulevard. Two words were tolling in his ears forlornly, an echo from romantic ballads of the West Indies: far overseas, far overseas. Cats slunk by furtively along the gutters. "No," he said to himself, "that bearded squireen won't have outsiders poaching on his preserves." Still, he was getting to understand Ramèges better; the man was not (as Claude had first believed) guided by self-interest. He stood up for the established order not so much against another's project as against a temperament wholly alien from his own. And he was standing up at the same time for the prestige of his Institute.

"Still," Claude reflected, "even for his own sake, he should try to get out of me all I can supply him with, since it's quite obvious that his present assistants won't risk their skins up there. He's behaving like a company director building up reserves. 'In thirty years' time . . .' and so forth. But, in thirty years' time, will his Institute still exist, or the French still hold this colony . . . far overseas? He may even think that if the men he sent out there are dead, they died just that his colleagues might carry on their jobs—though, of course, neither of them died for his precious Institute! If, in his heart of hearts, he is defending a group-interest, he'll turn nasty, that's sure. And, if he thinks he's standing up for the men who died, he'll be furious with me. Well, it's up to me to foresee the tricks he'll try. . . ."

4

Sitting in the cabin of the launch which was to take
them on shore, Claude saw Perken's face silhouetted
against a window, as he had so often seen it on the
liner outlined against a port-hole during meals.
Behind them the white river-steamer which had
brought them by night from Pnom-Penh rode at an-
chor. The region where Perken's old friend had disappeared was not far from the Royal Way, which
followed more or less the border of the unpacified
tracts, and such information as Claude had been able
to glean by discreet enquiries at Bangkok had confirmed the feasibility of their scheme.

The launch cast off and threaded its way between

trees rooted in the water; branches coated with
slime caked by the heat, and veined with streaks of
mud, scraped against the windows. On the tree-
trunks rings of dried froth marked the high-water
limit of the spate. Here was the prologue to the jungle life that lay before him, and Claude could not
take his eyes off the scene. The fumes of warm mud
simmering in the sun and the rancid odor of drying
scum and decaying animal matter assailed his nostrils, and his eyes were fascinated by the curious flac-
cid bodies of the small amphibians clustered on the
branches. Beyond the leafy barrier, through each
gap, he strained to catch a glimpse of Angkor-Wat
and its towers soaring above the tree-trunks bent
awry by the lake-breezes; but in vain. The leaves,
reddened by the sunset glow, shrouded the fenlands
with a glowing pall. The atmosphere of decay reminded him of something he had seen at Pnom-Penh:
a blind man chanting the Ramayana as he twanged
a primitive guitar. What better personification of
Cambodia, of this land of decay, could he have
found than that old singer whose heroic strains had
ceased to interest any but the beggars and coolie-
women squatting round him? Cambodia, a land possessed, and tamed to humble uses, its ancient hymns,
like its temples, fallen on evil days; of all dead lands
most dead. He glanced again at the swarm of hideous insects squirming in their muddy shells amongst
the branches. . . . And, on the nearing shore,

58

loomed darkly hostile, like a clenched fist, the jungle.

At last the launch touched land. A Ford car plying for hire was waiting on the bank. A young native stepped forward and addressed the captain.

"That's your chap," the captain said to Claude.

"The 'boy'?"

"Yes. I can't say if he's up to much, but he's the only servant to be got at Siem-Reap."

Perken asked the boy the stock questions, and engaged him.

"Take my tip, don't give him an advance of pay," shouted the captain, who had gone a little distance from them.

With a slight shrug of his shoulders the native sat down beside the driver of the white men's car, which started off at once. Another car followed with the kit.

"To the bungalow?" the driver asked without looking round. The car had swung into a straight road and was gaining speed.

"No. To the Residency first."

The forest streamed past on either hand; outlined against the red surface of the road before them, they saw the boy's smooth-shaven head. The chirring of the cicadas was so shrill as to be audible above the rattle of the engine. The driver waved his hand towards a sudden glimpse of the horizon. "There's Angkor-Wat," he shouted. But in the twilight Claude could not see more than twenty yards ahead.

At last a glow of fires and lamps lit up the foreground, speckled by dark moving forms of chickens and black pigs. The village was in sight. Presently the car pulled up.

"This Deputy Resident's bungalow?"

"Yessir!"

"I shan't be more than a minute or two, I expect," Claude said to Perken.

The Deputy Resident received him in a high-roofed room. Going up to Claude he shook his outstretched hand so slowly that he seemed to be judging its weight.

"Very glad to see you, Monsieur Vannec, glad to see you. Been expecting you some time, you know. The damned boat was late, of course—as per usual."

He spluttered out his greeting through a thick white moustache, without releasing Claude's hand. The shadow of his massive nose botched the corner of a Cambodian painting on the wall.

"So that's the great idea—eh?—a jungle jaunt?"

"I presume, sir, that as you have been informed of my arrival you know the nature of the research I am intended to undertake."

"You are 'intended'—that's a good one!—'intended to undertake'! Well, well, it's your own look-out!"

"I assume I can count on your assistance in getting the supply warrants for my transport duly executed?"

As the old official rose from his chair without replying his joints creaked in the silence. He started pacing up and down the room, followed by his shadow.

"Better keep on the move like I do, Monsieur Vannec, if you don't want to be eaten alive by the damned 'squitos. It's the worst time of day for them, you know. About the supply warrants, hm, hm. . . ."

(That trick he has of grunting is getting on my nerves, Claude thought. Wish he'd drop acting the grim old wardog!)

"Yes?" Claude asked. "What about them?"

"Well, it's like this. . . . You'll get 'em right enough, don't you worry! Only, you know, those sort of things don't cut much ice in these parts. Oh, I know the fellows they send out on research work don't like to be told their business; it puts their back up, of course. Still . . ."

"Yes?"

"Well, you know, what you're out to do isn't an easy little jaunt like the other fellows had. See here, I may as well tell you straight out—supply warrants in these parts, they're in a manner of speaking just a . . . a washout."

"So I shan't get anything?"

"No, that's not what I mean. You're sent out on an exploring job; well and good, there's no getting behind that. You'll be given everything you need to be given; don't you fret about that part of it. Orders are orders, as they say. Though, as far as *you're* concerned, things aren't quite so rosy as they look."

"Meaning?"

"Well I guess you know I'm not paid to give away their secrets to you or anybody else. But, damn it all, there's some things in this lousy job of mine I just can't stomach. No, I don't believe in looking for trouble. So, see here, young man, I'm going to give you a tip, a pretty useful tip—straight from the horse's mouth, what? Call off your jungle trip! Take my advice and cut it out! Go back to one of the big towns, Saigon, for instance. And wait there a bit. And, mind you, I know what I'm talking about."

"Do you think I've come half way round the world just to twiddle my thumbs in Saigon, like a nice, well-behaved little tourist?"

"As for coming half way round the world, we've all of us done that in our time, only we don't brag about it. But that's just what puzzles me; seeing the trouble you've taken, why couldn't you have fixed things up properly with Monsieur Ramèges and his —what d'you call it?—Institute? That would have been far better for everyone all round, and I shouldn't have been mixed up in a nasty business. Of course, what I've been telling you . . ."

"I am much obliged, my dear sir, for your advice —it proves your good will towards me"—"or your ill will towards the Institute," he almost added. "But, on the other hand, you assure me that, in any case, no obstacles will be placed in the way of my venture, and I hardly think that . . ."

"I said nothing of the kind. I said you'd get whatever you're entitled to."

"Ah, yes. I think I'm beginning to see daylight. But, all the same, I'd like . . ."

"To know more about it? Well, let me tell you right away; your curiosity won't be satisfied. Now let's get down to facts. Will you think it over?"

Claude shook his head.

"You're set on going on with it?"

"Quite."

"Very well. Let's hope you've got good and sufficient reason for carrying on—otherwise, Monsieur Vannec, if you'll excuse my saying so, you'll be making a fool of yourself. Well then, I'd better give you —no, that can wait; I've something to tell you about this fellow Perken."

"What?"

"I've got . . . let's see, it must be in the other file. No? Well, it's all the same; somewhere or other I've a memorandum from the Cambodian Secret Service, and I'm to convey the contents to you. Make no mistake; if I'm telling you about it, it's because I've got instructions. Personally, you know, I've no use for that sort of bunkum. Damn silly, I call it. There's only one thing that matters in these parts and that's the timber trade. They'd much better give me some help in carrying on my job efficiently than pestering me with all that dope about old rocks and stones."

"Well?"

"This is it. This chap Perken who's traveling with you was given his passport only because the Siamese Government insisted on it. He's going to look for a fellow called Grabot, or so he says. Mind you, they could have refused to give him a passport, as Grabot's a deserter from the army."

"Well, why didn't they? Not out of kindness of heart, I imagine?"

"Over here we've got to clear up getaways of that sort. Anyhow this man Grabot's a bad egg, one of the worst. He was a marked man, more or less, before he lit out."

"Perken knew him only very slightly, I believe. But what's that got to do with me?"

"Perken's a sort of high official in Siam—well, not really an official; can't say exactly what he is. I know him; I've been hearing things about him for the last ten years. And (this is between ourselves) when he went to Europe he started negotiations with us—not with the Siamese, mind you—for buying some machine-guns."

Claude stared at the man without speaking.

"So that's how the land lies, Monsieur Vannec. Well, when do you want to start?"

"As soon as possible."

"Then, let's say, in three days' time. You'll have what you need at 6 A.M. Got a boy?"

"Yes. He's in the car."

"I'll come down with you and give him the neces-

sary orders right away. By the way, I've got some let-
ters for you."

He handed Claude some envelopes, one of which
bore the seal of the French Institute. Claude was
about to open it when the tone of the Deputy Resident's voice as he hailed the boy caused him to raise
his eyes. Under the portico lamp the car shone blue.
The boy who had moved away—when he saw the official approaching, most likely—came forward now,
reluctantly, it seemed. Some words passed between
them in the Annamese tongue; Claude watched their
faces with all the more attention as he did not understand the words. The boy seemed terrified, while the
Deputy Resident gesticulated, his moustache flashing
silver in the electric light.

"I must warn you that your boy has been in jail."

"What for?"

"Gambling, petty theft. You'd better look for another."

"I'll think about it."

"Anyhow I've explained things to him. If you sack
him, he'll—hm, hm—transmit my instructions to his
successor."

After saying some more words in Annamese he
shook Claude's hand. From his gray, stubbly hair to
his canvas shoes, his white, unmoving form stood out
against the somber background of the forest. He
looked Claude in the eyes, opening and shutting his
mouth as if about to speak, and held his hand so long

65

that the young man wondered if he had some further message to impart. Then, abruptly, he let his hand fall to his side and, with another little grunt, stepped back into the bungalow.

"Boy!"

"Sir?"

"What's your name?"

"Xa."

"Did you hear what the Deputy said about you?"

"Sir, he not speaking true."

"True or not, I don't care a damn! Do you understand? *I don't care*. If you do your duty by me, the rest doesn't matter. Savvy?"

The boy stared at Claude, dumbfounded.

"Got it?"

"Yessir."

"Right. And did you hear what the captain said?"

"Master not to give advance."

"Well, here are five piasters. . . . Off you go, driver!"

Claude took his seat in the car.

"A system of yours?" Perken enquired with a smile.

"Call it that if you like," Claude replied. "If he's a scoundrel he'll have skedaddled by to-morrow; if not, he's dependable from now on. Loyalty, in my view, is one of the rare sentiments that haven't gone rotten nowadays."

"Perhaps. . . . And what had that grouchy old warrior got to say for himself?"

"Some rather queer things," Claude answered after a moment's reflection. "I'll have to tell you about them. However, to begin with essentials: we shall have our carts the day after to-morrow. But he hinted pretty clearly that I'd be well advised to go straight back to Saigon."

"What for?"

"For . . . nothing! That's as far as he'll go. It looks as if he doesn't relish the orders he's received; but he's going to carry them out."

"You couldn't find out anything more about them?"

"No. Unless . . . Wait a bit!"

The sealed envelope was still in his hand. He had some trouble opening it and, when he had extracted the letter, could not see to read it. Perken produced his electric torch.

"Stop!" Claude shouted to the driver.

The rattle of the engine died down, was lost in the hum of the cicadas.

"'*Dear Sir,*'" Claude read aloud, "'*I feel it incumbent on me*'—a good start, that!—'*with a view to enabling you to keep the persons who may accompany you under proper surveillance, to bring to your notice the Order of the Governor-General, herewith enclosed, a regulation still in force, the purport of which, if somewhat indefinite as it stands, will be defined more precisely in a subsequent administrative order to be issued in a few days' time. With my best wishes*'—that's all; no, wait! Listen to this!—'*my*'

67

best wishes for the success of your venture, very sincerely yours. . . .' What's the Order?"

He scanned the second sheet of paper. *" 'The Governor-General of Indo-China, on the motion of the Director of the French Institute'*—to hell with him!—*'issues the following General Order: It is hereby declared that all ancient edifices, whether already located or hereafter to be discovered, situate within the provinces of Siam-Reap, Battambang and Sisophon, shall be deemed to be monuments of public interest.'* It's dated 1908."

"That all?"

"The usual red tape! Not worth stopping for on so good a road. Carry on, driver!"

"Well then?"

Perken turned the light of the electric torch on to Claude's face.

"Put it out, please. Why do you say 'well then'? You surely don't suppose that's going to change my plans?"

"I'm glad to be right in thinking it won't change them. That was just the sort of reaction I expected from your Government—I told you so on the boat. The job will be a stiffer one, that's all. Still, once we're in the jungle . . ."

Claude was so convinced of the impossibility of turning back that the mere notion of discussing ways and means exasperated him. The great adventure had begun—so much the better. He would have no truck with doubts; the one thing to do was to forge ahead, like the car boring its way through the darkness, across the welter of the forest. The sudden shadow of a horse swerved from the headlights. Electric lamps showed up ahead: the bungalow.

While the boy attended to their kit, Claude, without so much as waiting to order a drink, swept aside the back numbers of illustrated papers that littered the rattan table, and, oblivious to a buzzing swarm of mosquitoes, began to unscrew the cap of his fountain-pen.

"Surely you're not answering him at once?" Perken asked.

"Don't worry, I won't send the letter till we're starting off. But I'll write my answer; that will calm my nerves. It won't be long, anyhow."

Short enough; four lines all told. He handed the sheet to Perken while writing the address.

"Dear Sir,

Also the fabled bearskin of the uncaught bear is hereby declared a monument of public interest; but it might be rash to come and hunt for it.

> *Still more sincerely yours,*
>
> *Claude Vannec."*

The bungalow attendant tentatively produced some bottles of soda-water.

"Let's have a drink and then go for a stroll," Claude suggested. "The day's not over yet."

The spacious causeway leading to the temple of Angkor-Wat started on the far side of the road; they began to walk along it. At every step their shoes

69

caught in the dislocated paving-stones. Perken sat down on a stone block.

"Well?"

Claude repeated the conversation he had had with the Deputy Resident. Perken lit a cigarette; for a moment his gaunt, weather-beaten features, illumined by the tiny flame, glimmered in the darkness; then his face faded out behind the red glow of his burning cigarette.

"So that's all the Deputy Commissioner had to tell you about me," was his only comment.

"Quite enough, I should say."

"And what did you think of it all?"

"Nothing. We're risking our lives together; I'm here to help you, not to call you to account. If you want machine-guns my only regret is that you didn't tell me so before, as I'd have liked to help you get them."

The vast silence of the forest closed down on them once more, heavy with the fumes of new-turned earth. Strident as a slaughtered pig's last squeal, somewhere a bullfrog croaked and echoes crowded out the silence, dying away into the darkness, across the fetid emanations of the fens. Claude went on speaking.

"Let's get it clear. When I join forces with a man I take him as I find him—just as I take myself, without reserve. Once the two of us are comrades, how dare I say of any act he's done that I should not myself have done it?"

Again a silence intervened. Perken spoke at last.

"You've never been seriously . . . let down, so far?"

"It's always dangerous—thinking against mass-opinion. But to whom should I turn if not to those who, like myself, are always on the defensive?"

"Or on the offensive."

"Or on the offensive. Exactly."

"And don't you worry about the situations in which such friendships may involve you?"

"Must I fight shy of love because of syphilis? . . . I won't say I never worry over them; but I take them as they come."

In the darkness Perken laid his hand on Claude's shoulder.

"For your sake, Claude, I hope you will die young. I wish it as I've wished for few things in my life. You've no idea what it means to be imprisoned in one's own life; I began to get some inkling of it only when we parted, Sarah and I. It made no difference to me that whenever a man's mouth caught her fancy she slept with him (especially during the periods when she was left to herself)—just as she would have followed me, if needs be, to the convict prison—and she'd been through no end of experiences in Siam after her marriage with Prince Pitsanulok. A woman who knew much of life, nothing of death. One day she saw her life had settled into a groove, become involved in mine. And then she began to loathe the sight of me, as she loathed her mirror. (You know the eyes a woman has when her glass tells her once again that the tropics will soon have stamped her face indelibly with the 'malaria mask'—know what I mean?) Then all the hopes she'd cherished as a girl began, like a dose of syphilis caught in early youth, to eat away her life—and, by contagion, mine as well. You can't imagine what it means: that feeling of being penned in by destiny, by something you can't escape or change, something that weighs upon you like a prison regulation; the certainty that you will do *this* and nothing else, and when you die you will have been *that* man and no other, and what you haven't had already you will never have. And all your hopes lie behind you, all those baffled hopes that are flesh of your flesh, as no human being, living or to be born, can ever be."

An odor of corruption wafted from the stagnant marshes hung on the air. A picture rose before Claude's eyes: his mother wandering forlornly through his grandfather's old house, almost invisible in the half-light but for the bulge of her heavy hair dully glinting in the gloom; he saw her peering into the little mirror crested with a galleon in full sail, staring aghast at the sagging corners of her lips and her swollen nose, stroking her eyelids with blind, automatic gestures.

"I understood her," Perken went on. "I had nearly reached that stage myself—the time for settling up accounts with hope. It's like having to murder someone for whose sake one has always lived. As easy, and as cheerful! I don't suppose you can understand what that means, killing somebody who doesn't want to die. When a man has no children, has never wanted children, there's no question of passing on his hopes; the only thing he can do is to murder them himself. That's why one can have so deep a sympathy for someone who, one discovers, shares the same hopes. . . ."

Monotonously rising, overtone on overtone, the chorus of the frogs droned through the darkness, on and on towards a far, invisible horizon.

"Youth is a religion which, in the long run, a man has always to retract. And yet—! I made a serious attempt to do what Mayrena tried to do, when he fancied himself an actor on the stage of one of your French theaters. Just to *be* a king means nothing; it's the building up of a kingdom that's worth while. I didn't act the fool with saber-duels, and though, believe me, I'm a good shot, I hardly ever used my rifle. But I'm in close relations with almost all the chiefs of the unpacified tribes as far as Upper Laos. Fifteen years I've been at it, tackling them one after the other, brave men and sots. And now it's I whom they look up to, not the Siamese Government."

"What do you want to make of them?"

"I *wanted* . . . First of all, a military force; a crude one, perhaps, but easy to bring up to scratch in a very short time. And then to await the struggle that's bound to come out here, either between the settlers and the natives, or between the Europeans themselves. Then I could set on foot the great adventure. You see, I want to survive for many men, and perhaps for a long time; to leave my mark upon the map of Asia. In the great game I'm playing against death I'd rather have twenty tribes to back me than a child. . . . Yes, that was what I wanted, just as my father coveted his neighbor's land—or I want women."

The tone in which he spoke the last words came as a surprise to Claude; it was quite unemotional, cool and collected, without the least trace of obsession.

"Why don't you want it now?" Claude asked.

"Now I want—peace."

He uttered the word "peace" as if he had said "action." Though his cigarette was lit, he had not snapped to the lighter. Holding it near the wall, he examined minutely the carvings and the grooves between the stones; it almost seemed as if he looked to find his "peace" there.

"No," Perken said at last, "we couldn't remove anything from a wall like this one."

He extinguished the tiny flame and the wall sank back into an intense darkness faintly mottled above their heads by wavering gleams—joss-sticks, most likely, burning before the Buddhas. A hemisphere of stars was blotted out by the huge mass squatting in front of them, whose unseen imminence they felt brooding upon the shadows.

"Can you smell the mudflats?" Perken continued. "My scheme's like them: rotten and corrupted. It's

74

gone stale on me. Before two years are out the extension of the railroad will have been completed, and within five years they'll have pushed their roads or railroads right across the jungle."

"What's your quarrel with the roads? Their strategical importance?"

"They haven't any. No, what with alcohol and cheapjack wares, my Mois will go to the dogs. Nothing doing. I'll have to kowtow to the Siamese, or else throw up the sponge."

"And your machine-guns?"

"In the region where I live I'm still my own master and, if I could get arms, I'd hold out there until my death. And then . . . there are the women. Yes, if I'd a few machine-guns I could hold the region against an army corps, unless they were ready to sacrifice any number of lives."

Claude wondered: did the railroad lines, as yet unfinished, suffice to explain Perken's attitude? It was little likely that the jungle tribes could withstand the impact of so-called civilization, with its advance-guard of Annamites and Siamese. And "the women," he had said; Claude had not forgotten Djibouti.

"So it was only considerations of that sort put you off your scheme?"

"I haven't done with it. If an opportunity comes . . . But I can't devote my whole life to it any longer. Not that I haven't thought of it a lot—after that fiasco at the Djibouti brothel, too. Really what's put me off it, as you say, is . . . my failures with women. It's not impotence; don't run away with that idea. Just a hint, a menace. Like the first time I noticed Sarah growing old. The end of something. Above all, I feel my hopes have been drained away, and some dark force, a sort of hunger, is getting hold of me, fighting me down."

Somewhere in the depths of Claude's consciousness his passionate avowal struck an answering note, and Perken knew it.

"I've never given much thought to money. The Siamese Government owe me more than I'll ever claim; but there's nothing to be got out of them now. They mistrust me too much. Not that they've any specific reason for doing so; they mistrust me in a general way, much as I mistrust the next two or three years, during which I've got to keep my hopes in storage. One should tackle jobs like that without having to depend on state assistance, and having to play the part of a hunting dog who bides his time to hunt on his own account. But no one's ever brought it off, or, for that matter, made a serious attempt at it. Not even Brooke in Sarawak, not even Mayrena. Schemes like mine are in a bad way when you've got to pause and think out what they're worth. Looks as if I'd staked my life on a venture too big for me."

"What else could you do?" Claude asked.

"Nothing. But that venture masked the rest of the world from me, and, on occasion, I've needed that pretty badly. If I'd put it through, my scheme . . .

But I don't give a damn if all my ideas are so much hogwash, so long as there are women."

"Women's bodies?"

"It's hard to realize all the loathing of the world that lies behind that thought: 'one woman more.' Each body that one hasn't yet possessed is—an enemy. . . . And nowadays I've all my old dreams to goad me on. . . ."

Like the vast fane before them, looming through the night, the dark insistence of his mood lay heavy on Claude's thoughts.

"And then—only try to grasp all that this country really is. Why, I'm only just beginning to understand their erotic rites, the process of assimilation by which a man comes to identify himself, even in his sensations, with the woman he possesses—till he imagines *he is she,* yet without ceasing to be himself! There's nothing in the world to match it—sensual pleasure strained to the point when it becomes intolerable, the breaking-point of pain! No, for me these women aren't merely bodies; they're . . . instruments. And I want . . ." Claude guessed his unseen gesture, the gesture of a hand crushing out life. ". . . as I once wanted to conquer men."

What he's really after, Claude mused, is self-annihilation. I wonder is he more aware of it than he admits. Anyhow he'll achieve it easily enough. Perken had spoken of his frustrated hopes in a tone implying that he had not wholly given them up; or,

77

if he had abandoned them, that his "eroticism" was not their only compensation.

"I haven't done with my men yet. From where I shall be I'll be able to keep an eye on the Mekong—it's a pity I don't know the region where we're going, or you don't know of another Royal Way two hundred miles further up-country—but I mean to look after it myself, and have no neighbors. Yes, we've got to find out what's become of Grabot."

"Where exactly did he go?"

"Somewhere near the Dang-Reks, thirty miles off the route we're going to take. Why did he go there? His Bangkok pals swear he was after gold; every ne'er-do-well from Europe has gold on the brain. But he knows the country, he can't have fallen for that sort of yarn. I've heard rumors, too, of a scheme he had of trading piece-goods with the unpacified tribes."

"How do they pay?"

"With skins or, sometimes, gold-dust. Yes, a trading scheme's more likely. He's from Paris; I can see his father as an inventor of patent tie-clips, self-starters, tap-nozzles and that sort of gadget. But I fancy his main reason for going there was to settle things up with himself. (I'll tell you about that some other time.) Anyhow the Bangkok Government was certainly behind his venture, or they wouldn't be so keen on finding out what's become of him. He probably went there on their account, and now he's playing some game of his own—a bit too soon in my opinion. Otherwise he'd keep them posted. Perhaps they'd told him to find out what I was up to in those parts. As a matter of fact, he set out while I was away."

"But he didn't go to the same part of the country as you, did he?"

"If he had, he'd have been greeted on his arrival with arrows and, what's more, a bullet or two from my Gras rifles. No, he couldn't have gone there direct. If he meant to explore those parts he must have tried to get through by the Dang-Rek country."

"What sort of man is he?" Claude asked.

"Listen to this! During his military service he fell foul of an M.O. who'd refused him sick-leave when he was really ill; so I've heard, but it may have been something quite different. Next week he reported sick again and went to the infirmary. 'That you again? Got a bad tooth, eh? Let's have a look at it!' Grabot opened his hand—and there was an old dog's tooth in it! A month's cells for that. He wrote to the General at once, complaining of ophthalmia. No sooner was he in the lock-up—I forgot to tell you he had a dose of blennorhoea at the time—than he began scraping off the pus and rubbing it into an eye. Well, he got the M.O. told off all right, but it cost him an eye. He's never got back his sight in it. He's one of your bullet-headed Frenchmen, with a potato nose and a great hulking body like a navvy's. He always created a sensation whenever he entered one of the Bangkok pubs—and didn't he love it! Worth seeing it was, the way the other fellows used to watch him from the corner of an eye and edge away as he slouched up to the corner where his pals were, holding up their glasses to him and bawling at the top of their voices. He's a deserter from one of your African battalions. Grabot's another one who's had some queer dealings with eroticism."

Part Two

1

For four days past they had seen nothing but the forest. Even the villages near which they camped seemed bred of the forest like their wooden Buddhas and palm-thatched huts asquat like monstrous insects on the spongy soil. In the glaucous sunlight, dense as the sheen of an aquarium, every thought grew turbid, decomposed. On their path they had encountered some small, dilapidated shrines, their stones so tightly swathed in claw-like roots that clamped them to the ground that they seemed not the work of human hands but of some extinct species, inured to a life without horizons and the dim sea-depths of the virgin forest. Obliterated by the passing centuries, the Way revealed its old alignment only by occasional mounds of festering rubble, the sudden glint of a toad's eyes as it crouched, unmoving, in a nook between the stones. Did they imply success or failure —these vestiges strewn along the Way like corpses of the forest's victims? Would they reach at last the sculptured temple to which they were being led by a young native who never ceased smoking Perken's cigarettes? Three hours ago they should have made it; but the heat and the never-ending forest harassed them even more than their anxiety. Like a slow poison, the ceaseless fermentation in which forms grew bloated, lengthened out, decayed, as in a world where mankind has no place, wore down Claude's stamina insidiously; under its influence, in the green darkness, he felt himself disintegrating like the world around him. And then, everywhere, the insects. . . .

Elusive, rarely visible, the other animals came from a cleaner world where the high foliage did not, as here, seem glued by viscid air to the moist leaves on which the horses trod; they belonged to that more human universe glimpses of which appeared now and again in a burst of dazzling sunlight, a blaze of sparkling motes, traversed by the sudden shadows of swift birds. But the insects lived by and on the forest—from the globular black creatures which the draught-oxen squashed under their hooves, and the ants zig-zagging up the porous tree-trunks, to the spiders hooked by grasshopper-like claws to the centers of their huge webs, four yards across, whose silken filigree caught up the light that lingered near the

84

soil and masked the formless tangle of the undergrowth with never-changing forms of shining sym-
metry. Amid the welter of the leafage heaving with
scaly insects only the spiders kept steadfast vigil, yet
some vague resemblance linked them, too, with the
other insects—the flies and cockroaches, the curious
little creatures with heads protruding from their
shells crawling upon the moss—, with the foul viru-
lence of bacterial life seen on a microscopic slide.
The high gray anthills, on whose surface the termites
never showed themselves, towered up through the
dusk like mountain-peaks on some dead satellite;
they seemed bred of the corruption of the air, the
stench of fungus, the swarms of tiny leeches glued
together like flies' eggs beneath the leaves. Claude
was growing aware of the essential oneness of the
forest and had given up trying to distinguish living
beings from their setting, life that moves from life
that oozes; some unknown power assimilated the
trees with the fungoid growths upon them, and
quickened the restless movements of all the rudimentary creatures darting to and fro upon a soil like
marsh-scum amid the steaming vegetation of a planet
in the making. Here what act of man had any meaning, what human will but spent its staying power?
Here everything frayed out, grew soft and flabby,
tended to assimilate itself with its surroundings,
which, loathsome yet fascinating as a cretin's eyes,
worked on the nerves with the same obscene power
of attraction as the spiders hanging there between

the branches, from which at first it had cost him such an effort to avert his gaze.

Soundlessly the ponies moved ahead, with lolling necks; the young guide led the way slowly but unfalteringly, followed by Svay, the Cambodian whom the Resident had sent with the party to see they got their cartmen—and to spy on their doings. Just as Claude glanced behind him with a quick jerk of his neck—for a morbid fear of blundering into a spider's web made him keep anxious watch ahead—he started at a sudden contact. Perken had touched his arm and was pointing with a cigarette that in the murky air glowed fiery red, towards a dark mass whence canes were sprouting here and there, half hidden in the forest. Once again Claude's eyes had failed to pierce the close-set maze of tree-trunks.

Before him lay the ruins of a brown-stone wall, stippled with patches of moss. Despite the heat some tiny dewdrops were sparkling on it still like diamonds. "That must be the precinct wall," he said to himself; "obviously the moat's been filled up."

The track soon disappeared. Pushing their way round a heap of rubble, they came upon a clump of cane-brake, interlaced like wattles, which, rising to a man's height, formed a natural palisade between the ruins and the forest. The boy shouted to the cartmen to bring their wood-knives; his voice rang dead, stifled by the canopy of leaves. Claude felt his fingers contracting like the excavator's, as he grips his crowbar, delving beneath the surface for some hidden booty. Forward and down the cartmen's shoulders swayed in a slow, languid rhythm; then, with a sudden jerk, they straightened up again, while a blue glint of metal flashed above their heads, reflecting in a shining arc the unseen brightness of the sky. With each parallel swing of the blades from right to left Claude seemed to feel again a stinging in his arm— the needle of that abominable doctor of his boyhood, who, in his fumblings for the vein, had kept on scraping off the skin. As the track was cleared across the thicket by slow degrees, a reek of stagnant water filled the air, more fetid even than the forest. Perken followed the cartmen step by step. A dry cane splintered with a brittle click under his boot and two frogs hopped leisurely aside, while, above the tree-tops, some large birds flapped away on clumsy wings.

Now that the cartmen had cleared a track up to the wall, it seemed to Claude it should be easy to find the entrance-gate and take their bearings from it; as it was only to the left they could have deviated, all they had to do was to follow the circuit of the wall, bearing towards the right. Some canes and thorny bushes sprouted along the base of the wall. Claude stepped back, jumped, and landed on top of it.

"Can you walk along it?" Perken asked.

The wall cut through the foliage like a road, but it was coated with a slimy moss, and a fall might be a very serious matter, for gangrene is as prevalent as vermin in the jungle He decided not to walk upright. Lying flat, face downward, he began to wriggle forwards. The layer of moss was strewn with fallen leaves, some viscous, other frayed to the fiber as if the moss had gnawed them, and reeked of decay. Magnified by its proximity, the carpet of the moss lay level with his eyes, quivering incessantly though there was not a breath of wind; the tremor of the fronds betrayed the presence of unseen insects. After advancing thus three yards or so, he felt something tickling his neck.

Halting, he passed his fingers over his neck; the titillation moved on to his hand, which he withdrew at once. Two black ants, with waving feelers, as big as wasps, were trying to crawl between his fingers. Standing up, he shook his hand violently, and the insects fell off. He carefully inspected his clothes; no ants there, anyhow. At an extremity of the wall, a hundred yards ahead, there was a wide gap—the gate, presumably, where the sculpture would be found. The soil below was strewn with fallen stones. Before him he saw the overhanging branch of a tree, silhouetted across the gap; over the green bridge a troop of ants was passing, their bellies showing clearly against the light, their legs invisible. "Better shift that branch," Claude murmured, but failed to reach it at first. "Well, I've got to make the end of the wall somehow or other, though pretty foul it'll be if there are red ants about; worse, however, if I turned back. Still, I dare say they're not as deadly as all that. . . ."

"Well?" Perken shouted, but Claude did not reply at once. He took another step forward. Impossible to keep his balance. The wall seemed like a living creature, tugging at his hands. As he let himself down towards it, instinctively his muscles showed him the best way to walk: not on hands and knees, but on his hands and tiptoe (a picture flashed before his mind of an angry cat arching its back). He started forward at once. In this position either hand could protect the other, and as his feet and calves were sheathed in leather, his contact with the moss was reduced to a minimum.

"All's well!" he shouted back to Perken. The jerkiness of his voice, its unwonted shrillness, took him by surprise; all the disgust of his experience with the ants was in it. He moved forward slowly; it exasperated him to find his limbs so little under control, their movements so ungainly; to feel his loins swaying him right and left in desultory jerks instead of helping him to progress more quickly. He stopped again, one hand uplifted, like a pointing setter, arrested by a sensation which intense excitement had till now kept from his consciousness; something sticky was smeared upon his hand, a mush of brittle molluscs and tiny eggs squashed to a pulp. Once more his limbs seemed paralysed; his eyes took in only the flooding sunlight, but his nerves were conscious only of the mass of squashed insects, responded only to the nausea of their contact. Standing up, he spat, and glanced down for a second at the stones

89

below, teeming with insects; on those stones he might easily crush out his life. He dropped on to the wall once more, savagely, like a stampeded animal, and moved slowly on again, his sticky hands adhering to the rotten leaves, dazed with disgust and living only for the patch of light which drew him on towards it. Suddenly it seemed to explode, to burst into a blaze of open sky. Stupefied, he halted, crouching; for in his present position, on his hands and toes, he could not jump.

At last he managed to get a purchase on a corner of the wall and scrambled down.

Flagstones overgrown with grass led on towards another cone of darkness, to all appearances a solitary tower. Claude had seen the ground-plans of this type of shrine. Now that he could move like a man, he ran forward, shielding his head with his arms as well as might be, risking the chance of tearing his throat against the whiplash strands of rattan.

Useless to look for sculpture here; the temple was unfinished.

2

On their frustrated hope the forest had closed in
once more. For days the only ruins they had come
upon were of no account; like a river-bed, living and
dead at once, the Royal Way now disclosed only the
battered wreckage, the sun-bleached skeletons, which
racial migrations and invaders leave in their wake.
In the last village through which they had passed,
some wood-cutters spoke of a great building, the Ta-
Mean, which stood, they said, on the mountain crest
dividing the Cambodian marches from an unexplored region of Siam, in territory occupied by the
Moi tribe. They declared that in and about this
building were several hundred yards of bas-reliefs.

And, were it true, was not a desperately tantalizing

experience in store for them? "You couldn't remove a single stone from the walls of Angkor-Wat," Perken had said. Yes, that was obvious enough. Sweat beaded Claude's face, streamed down his body; sticky, intolerable sweat. In the depths of this forest, traversed only once a year by some ramshackle caravan bringing glassware to barter with the natives for sticklac and the local spices, no doubt his life might seem well worth a bullet. Still he did not believe that, without a prospect of substantial profit, marauders would dare attack armed Europeans. (Yet might not those marauders know of decorated temples?) All the same he was continually haunted by a feeling of uneasiness. "Am I getting fagged?" he wondered; and in that very second he realized that his gaze, idly ranging the tree-clad hillside which had just come into view across a break in the forest, was focused now on the smoke of a fire. For several days they had not met a soul.

There was no mistaking that the natives, too, had observed the smoke. All were staring at it, hunching their shoulders nervously, as if it portended disaster. Though there was not a breath of wind, Claude could distinctly smell an odor of scorched flesh. The oxen halted.

"Some wandering hill-tribe," Perken said. "If they're burning their dead it means there's a gathering of them over there." He drew his revolver. "But, if they are blocking the road . . ."

He plunged into the jungle growth, with Claude at

his heels. Keeping their hands pressed closely to their bodies for fear of the leeches which were beginning to fasten on their clothing, their fingers grasping their revolvers, they thrust their way through the brushwood. Neither spoke a word. Seeing the yellow-golden leafage of the trees suddenly become transparent, Claude guessed that they were near a clearing. The far side of the forest shone in the sun like a sheet of water. It was topped by slender palm-trees above which a dense column of smoke was rising slowly to the zenith. "For God's sake, keep under cover," Perken whispered. A distant clamor gave them their direction. Again Claude gasped at the smell—a smell of roasting meat. At the first opportunity he drew the branches apart. Above a line of bushes that partly blocked his view he saw a medley of thick-lipped faces and scintillating war-spears. A guttural dirge vibrated in the leaves and branches round them. In the center of the glade the thick white smoke could now be clearly seen, rising from a squat tower of wattles, at the top of which four wooden buffalo-heads, with horns the size of canoes, stood out against the sky. Leaning on the shaft of his flashing spear, scratching his head and bending towards the center of the pyre, a yellow warrior was gazing at the flames; he was stark naked, and in a state of erection. Claude, in his hiding-place, felt himself riveted to the sight—by his eyes, by his hands, by the leaves which seemed to touch him through his clothing, and, not least, by that feeling of panic which always used to come over him, as a child, whenever he saw a live crab or lobster, or a snake.

Perken had started back; Claude drew himself up at once, prepared to fire at a moment's notice. Whenever there was a lull in the rustling of the branches, the funeral chant was heard again, droning through the silence; it grew fainter and fainter as they retreated.

"Hey there! Get a move on!" Perken ordered gruffly as they rejoined the carts.

The clumsy vehicles lurched forward, their axles grinding out a hoarse arpeggio whose echo Claude could feel in every sinew. Now and again they had a glimpse of the smoke rising between the trees, a steady column in the windless air. Whenever they caught sight of it the natives urged on their beasts, crouching low over the cart-poles, as if some atavistic fear possessed them. Now and then, on the far side of a ravine, there appeared broad stretches of orange-colored rock to which the mass of trees below seemed straining up; the splashes of orange struck a violent contrast with the blue of the sky, which remained almost as intense as ever. Each time they came to an opening in the forest the cartmen glanced apprehensively towards the distant tree-tops, fearing to see another fire. But nothing flawed the calm blue horizon and the green canopy of leaves, over which the hot air swirled, as above a furnace, in great, rushing eddies.

Night fell, the dawn came, another night, another dawn, and at last they reached a remote village dithering with malaria, a village lost amid the universal disintegration of all things under an unseen sun. Now and then they caught sight of the mountains, and each time they loomed nearer. Low-growing branches swished noisily against the hoods of the carts, but even their intermittent rustle seemed muted by the heat. The warm miasma steaming up from the earth half suffocated them, but they had a consolation—the last guide's positive assurance that there was sculpture on the temple towards which they were proceeding.

But they had grown used to such affirmations. . . . For all his doubts regarding this temple—and indeed any specific temple they might go in quest of—Claude was held to his general idea of them by a half-skeptical belief, a complex of logical assurances and doubts so deep as to have become almost physiological. It was as if his eyes and nerves protested against his hope, against the unkept promises of this phantasmal road.

At last they reached a wall.

Claude's eyes were growing familiar with the forest. When near enough to discern the centipedes scurrying across the stonework, he realized that their guide had shown more intelligence than his predecessors and had led them to a fault which obviously marked the site of the former entrance. Like all the other temples this one was ringed by a tangled palisade of cane-brake. Perken, who was beginning to know the habits of the vegetation round such sites, pointed to a spot where the green barrier was less thick. "Pavement," he said. There, doubtless, was the pathway leading to the sanctuary. The cartmen set to work. With a noise like crumpled paper, the canes fell slowly right and left, leaving behind them tiny specks of white, shining like stars across the gloom— the pithy stumps slashed diagonally by the wood-knives. "If we don't find any sculpture or statues in this temple," Claude reflected, "what's to be done? None of the drivers will go with the three of us— Perken, myself and the boy—as far as the Ta-Mean. Ever since we ran into that wild tribe, they've had only one desire—to make a getaway. And, if there are only three of us, how are we to shift the two-ton blocks of which the big bas-reliefs are composed? Statues . . . possibly. And, of course, luck may come our way. But it's a damned silly business—silly as a boy's treasure-hunting yarn."

He took his eyes from the flashing wood-knives and looked down at the ground. The sliced canes were already turning brown. Why shouldn't he take a knife, too, and strike—more vigorously than those wretched jungle-wallahs? Couldn't he mow his way through the brake, using the knife like a scythe? A gentle touch from the guide drew him from his thoughts. A clump of canes had just been hacked away, revealing some smooth blocks—the gateway,

96

no doubt—speckled with the shadows of a few standing canes and ringed by fallen stonework.

Once again—sculptureless! The guide's lips were smiling; his forefinger still pointed to the gate. Never had Claude wanted so urgently to use his fists on a man's face. Clenching his hands, he turned to Perken —to find him smiling, too. Claude's friendship for his comrade turned suddenly to hate. Nevertheless, seeing them all staring at the same point, he followed the direction of their eyes. The main entrance had evidently been a large one and it began, not where he had expected, but on the far side of the wall. What all his companions, familiar with the forest, were looking at was one abutment of it, which stood up from the débris like a pyramid, on the apex of which was a sandstone figure, fragile but intact, crowned with a very delicately wrought diadem. Between the leaves he noticed a stone bird with outspread wings and a parrot's beak. A shaft of sunlight broke directly over one of its feet. All his anger vanished in that brief but splendid moment. Delight possessed him; he was filled with an aimless gratitude, with an elation which quickly yielded to a maudlin readiness to weep. Aware only of the sculpture, he moved blindly forward till he stood just in front of the gate. The lintel had fallen, bringing down all that was above it; branches festooned the standing uprights, forming a limp but massive archway, impervious to the sunlight. Beyond some heaps of fallen stones whose angles stood out black against the light and all but blocked the passage, a thin veil of flimsy wall-plants and slender sprays that ramified in veins of sap was stretched across the tunnel. Perken slashed through it, bringing into view a confused splendor, a haze of broken lights faceted by spiky aloe-leaves. Claude made his way along the passage from stone to stone, steadying himself against the sides; now and again he rubbed his hands against his trousers to remove the spongy feeling the moss had given them. Suddenly he recalled the ant-infested wall. There, too, a gap of brightness mottled with leafage had seemed to melt away into an opalescent glare, the universal majesty of light brooding above its kingdom of decay.

Before him lay a chaos of fallen stones, some of them lying flat, but most of them upended; it looked like a mason's yard invaded by the jungle. Here were lengths of wall in slabs of purple sandstone, some carved and others plain, all plumed with pendent ferns. Some bore a red patina, the aftermath of fire. Facing him he saw some bas-reliefs of the best period, marked by Indian influences—he was now close up to them—but very beautiful work; they were grouped round an old shrine, half hidden now behind a breastwork of fallen stones. It cost him an effort to take his eyes off them. Beyond the bas-reliefs were the remains of three towers razed to within six feet of the ground. Their mutilated stumps stuck out of such an overwhelming mass of rubble that all the vegetation round them was stunted; they seemed socketed in the débris like candles in their sticks. The shadows had shortened; an unseen sun was climbing up the sky. An imperceptible tremor, a perpetual vibration, began to stir within the leafy depths, though there was not the faintest breeze. The great heat was beginning.

A loose stone fell and sounded twice in falling, first with a muffled thud, then clearly; and Claude, in his mind's ear, caught an echo of the word: eer-ie. But it was not only the dead stones which the clumsy frogs quickened to fugitive life on this their first encounter with mankind, it was not only the utter desolation of this forsaken temple, nor was it but the veiled yet active malevolence of the vegetation that made the place seem so uncanny. Something inhuman brooded over all these ruins and the voracious plants which now seemed petrified with apprehension; a presence of numinous awe guarded with its dead hand these ancient figures holding their lonely court amongst the centipedes and vermin of the forest. Then Perken stepped past him, and in a flash the world of shimmering sea-depths died out, like a jelly-fish cast high and dry on the sea-shore; it lost its potency when faced by two white men.

"I'll fetch the tools," Perken said. His shadow swept down the tunnel between the tattered wall-plants.

It seemed that the main tower had completely collapsed only on one side, for three of its walls still

99

stood at the end of the biggest heap of débris. At some period a deep pit had been dug within these walls; after the Siamese incendiaries, treasure-hunters had evidently visited the spot. Now, plumb in the middle of the pit, there rose an anthill, dun-colored, with a pointed top; it also seemed to have been abandoned. Perken returned. He had a metal-cutting saw and a stick in his hand; from his bulging left-hand pocket a hammerhead projected. He drew from his pocket a quarryman's sledge and impaled it on the stick.

"Svay's in the village," he said, "I ordered him to stay there."

Claude had already picked up the saw. Its nickel frame shone brightly against the somber stonework. But, beside one of the walls which in its fall had formed a sort of staircase and on which a bas-relief was poised within his reach, he hesitated.

"What's the matter?" Perken asked.

"It's damned silly. . . . The fact is I've a feeling this isn't going to come off!"

He seemed to be seeing the stone for the first time, and could not rid himself of a sense of the disproportion between it and the saw he held. It made things seem impossible. However, he wetted the block and went at it with the saw, which bit into the sandstone with a shrill, rasping sound. At his fifth stroke it skidded; when he drew it from the fissure he found that all the teeth were gone.

They had a couple of dozen blades with them. The

notch he had made was little more than half an inch deep. He threw down the saw and stared into space. Many of the stones on the ground were faced with half-obliterated traces of bas-reliefs. In his obsession with the walls he had not noticed them. Possibly, he thought, such as had fallen face-downward might have kept the carved surfaces intact.

The same idea had already occurred to Perken. Calling the drivers up, he had them cut the trunks of some young trees into levers; with these they set about turning the blocks over. Each block was heaved slowly up till it toppled over, with a dull thud. On the side which now was uppermost, across a maze of tiny furrows traced by panic-stricken wood-lice in their flight, traces of sculptured figures were apparent. Then into each successive hollow, sharply indented as a plaster mold, whence the last block had been removed, another block was tipped over, and, one by one, the surfaces which ever since the epoch of the Siamese invasions had been moldering face-downward in the soil were once again exposed to daylight. The wavering criss-cross lines made by the insects as they scurried away into the forest suggested a stampede of frenzied Lilliputians. But the more Claude examined the shattered outlines of the fallen bas-reliefs, the clearer it became that the only stones worth removing were those composing one of the still standing sides of the main temple.

Carved on two faces, the corner-stones represented two dancing-girls. The figures extended over three stones, placed one on top of the other. It looked as if a vigorous push might bring the top one down.

"How much d'you think it's worth?" Perken asked.

"The two dancing-girls, you mean?"

"Yes."

"Hard to say. Over five hundred thousand francs anyhow."

"Sure?"

"Absolutely."

So, Perken mused, the machine-guns to buy which he had gone to raise the wind in Europe had been here all the time, here in the forest he knew so well, here in these stones! Were there any temples up in his own neighborhood? he wondered. They might, perhaps, serve him even better than machine-guns. If he could come upon a few such temples while he was "at home," he might impose his will on Bangkok, arming his men meanwhile. Each temple would mean ten machine-guns, two hundred rifles. . . . Looking at this temple, he forgot how many others had had no sculpture, forgot the Way. A picture held his eyes—his army on the march, sunlight glinting on the machine-gun barrels, the target sparkling in the sun.

Meanwhile Claude had been having the ground cleared of stones, so that the bas-relief should run no risk of being chipped when it fell. While the men were moving away the fallen blocks he examined the figures more attentively. A very light gray-blue moss, like the bloom on European peaches, covered one head, which, as was usual in Khmer statues, had smiling lips. Three men put their shoulders to the stone and pushed together. It overbalanced, fell edgewise, and sank into the earth deep enough not to roll over again. In being moved it had made two grooves in the stone on which it rested and along them two armies of dull-hued ants, intent on salvaging their eggs, were hurrying in Indian file. But the second stone, the top of which was now in view, had not been laid in the same way as the first. It was wedged into the main wall between two blocks, each of which weighed several tons. It looked as if, to get it out, the whole wall would need to be demolished, and that was obviously out of the question. If the stones faced with sculpture could only be handled with much difficulty, the other enormous blocks defied human powers. They must be left intact until the passing centuries or the peepul-trees sprouting in the ruins should lay them low.

How, he wondered, had the Siamese been able to wreck so many temples? There were tales of elephants harnessed in droves to the walls. . . . But he had no elephants. The only thing to do was to cut or break the stone so as to detach the sculptured face, whence the last ants were now retreating, from the part embedded in the wall.

Leaning on their improvised levers, the drivers waited. Perken produced his hammer and a chisel. The best way to set about splitting the stone was probably to chisel out a narrow groove in it. He began hammering. But, either because he handled the chisel inexpertly or because the sandstone was too hard, he only succeeded in chipping out the tiniest splinters. . . . And the natives would, no doubt, be clumsier still.

Claude could not stop staring at the stone. Against the background of trembling leaves and flecks of sunlight, it seemed immensely solid, sure of itself, instinct with ponderous malevolence. The grooves, the stone-dust flickered before his eyes. The last of the ants had vanished, without forgetting a single pulpy egg. Only the stone remained, impassive, self-willed as a living creature, able to say "No." A rush of blind rage swept over Claude and, planting his feet firmly on the ground, he pressed against the block with all his might. In his exasperation he looked round for some object on which to vent his anger. Perken watched him, his hammer poised in mid-air, with parted lips. Yes, Perken might know the jungle well, but all his forest-lore was useless here; these stones were a sealed book to him. Ah, had he only worked as a mason for six months! He wondered what to do. Should he get the men to pull on it, all together, with a rope? As well scratch it with his nails! And how could one get a rope round it? Yet, he felt, his life hung in the balance, in peril—yes, his very life. So all his obstinacy, his tense determination, the passionate endeavor which had urged him through the jungle had served no other end than this—to bring him up against this obstacle, an immovable stone planted between himself and Siam!

The more Claude stared at the stone, the more evident it became to him that they could never push through to the Ta-Mean with the carts. And, after all, the stones of the Ta-Mean could only be the same as these. His ardor to succeed was like hunger or thirst, an overwhelming impulse. It clenched his fingers round the hammer he had just snatched from Perken. In his rage he lashed out at the stone with all his might. Again and again the hammer sprang back with a brittle click that sounded grotesquely futile in the silence. Then the sun glinted on the polished claw-end of the hammer. Pausing, he stared at it for a second. Then, as if afraid that his idea might somehow escape him, he hastily reversed the hammer and began striking again, with all his force, beside the gleaming notch gouged out by Perken's chisel. A stone splinter several inches long sprang out. Dropping the hammer, he rubbed his eyes. Luckily they had only been struck by flying stone-dust. As soon as his sight came back, he put on his glare-glasses. Then he fell to hammering again. The claw-head was effective. Using it directly, he could strike the stone harder and much oftener than if a chisel were interposed. Each blow dislodged a large flake. In a few hours . . .

Meanwhile the cane-brake blocking the ways of access to the shrine had to be cleared away. Perken took a turn with the hammer. Claude went a little distance away with the cartmen to see about clearing a track. As he watched them at work he could hear the brisk clang of the hammer ringing out at rapid intervals above the soft swish of the falling reeds. It reminded him of a Morse telegraphist transmitting. In the vast silence of the forest, in the brooding heat, it had a human, an oddly trivial sound.

When he returned he found the earth around covered with flakes of stone piled round a cone of dust; the color of the dust surprised him. It was white, notwithstanding that the sandstone from which it came was purple. When Perken turned towards him, Claude noticed that the groove, like the stone-dust, was a brilliant white, and a wide one, for it was impossible always to strike in the same place.

He took over. Perken went on with the task of getting a fairway cleared. It would be a difficult business shifting the blocks; the simplest way would be to roll them over like logs, once all the pebbles had been removed from the track. Yard by yard the trail lengthened out along a vista of straight-falling shadows. In the yellowing light, the growing heat, the ever shorter shadows, one thing alone remained unchanged, the sound of steady hammer-blows. The heat was not merely oppressive, overpowering; it worked like a slow poison, turning their muscles to water, sapping their vitality, while the sweat poured down their faces, mingling with the stone-dust below their glasses in long, viscous streaks like bloodstreams trickling from gouged-out eyes. Claude hammered away almost mechanically, as a man lost in the desert goes walking on and on. His mind had gone to pieces, fallen in ruins like the temple; all that kept it still alive was the thrill of counting each successive hammer-stroke. That, anyhow, was one more; and that, one more again. The forest, the temple, the universe were in dissolution. He might have been struggling to bore through a prison wall, and the hammer-thuds have been so many thrusts of a file, rasping persistently against the stone.

Then suddenly there was a blank; everything fell into place, as if his world had caved in over him. He stood motionless, bewildered. Noticing that the sound of hammering had ceased, Perken stepped back a few paces. Then he saw that the two claws of the hammerhead had just broken off.

He ran up, snatched the hammer from Claude; for a moment he thought of filing the broken end into a new pair of claws, then, seeing how impossible that was, he lashed out blindly at the stone as Claude had done a little while ago. At last he sat down, and forced himself to take stock of the situation. They had several spare hammer-handles with them, but had not thought of buying an extra head.

Once he was able to shake off his feeling of catastrophe, Claude brought his mind back to the train of thoughts which had preoccupied him before he had conceived the idea of using the claw-hammer direct. That notion had come to him in a flash; might not

107

some other happy inspiration strike him now? But now he was in danger of succumbing to sheer physical exhaustion and a mood of supine hopelessness—the inertia of a worn-out animal. Ah, how good it would be to lie down, to sleep! The very vigor of the effort he had put forth helped the forest now to re-assert its prison-like dominion. He felt an impulse to let things take their course, to abrogate his will, even his body. Throb by throb, his blood seemed ebbing away. He pictured himself, his arms hugging his chest, like a man stricken by malaria, his body curled up like a sleeping animal; he would lose consciousness utterly, yielding with sublime relief to the reiterated call of heat and jungle. Then suddenly a surge of terror impelled him to renew the struggle. The stone-dust softly trickling bright and white as salt from the triangular notch cut in the stone was falling like the sand in an hour-glass, emphasizing the hugeness of the block. And, as he gazed at it, suddenly the block of stone regained its semblance of a living creature, gigantic, indestructible. It held his gaze imprisoned. His hate linked him to it as to an active enemy who barred his way and mounted guard on him, a predatory monster strong with the driving force which for months past had been the mainspring of his life.

He made an effort to invoke his intellect, enervated though it now was by long days in the jungle. But intellect had ceased to function in his life; merely to live was all. The opiates of the forest had numbed his brain and it was blind instinct that launched him once more against the stone.

Gritting his teeth, he took his stand in front of it. Watching the notch out of the corner of his eye, as if it were a beast about to spring, he picked up the hammer and, giving it a full swing round his body, brought it down on the block. The stone-dust began to flow again. He stared with fascinated eyes at the bright stream. His hate grew concentrated on the dust. Keeping his eye on it, he struck ringing blows; his chest and arms seemed welded to the sledge and his whole body swayed to and fro, like a heavy pendulum. All his awareness was centered in his arms and loins. His life, the hopes that had inspired him for the past year, his present sense of failure, all were fused in rage; they existed solely in the frenzied shock which thrilled him from head to foot each time he struck, whose stunning impact freed him from the thraldom of the jungle.

He paused to take breath. Perken was bending towards a corner of the wall.

"Wait a bit!" he said. "The stone we're having all this trouble with is the only one that's set in the wall. Look at the one below. It's loosely laid, like the first stone. Let's try to get it out first. Once we've done that our stone will have no direct support, and as the notch can't have improved its health . . ."

Claude called up two Cambodians and, while they pushed, tugged at the nether stone with all his might. It would not budge. The earth and the small plants

109

surrounding it were holding it back. He remembered that Khmer temples have no foundations, and had a trench dug round and underneath the stone, to loosen it. The natives worked quickly and well while they were digging round the stone, but, for the excavation, they took their time; obviously they feared the block might crush their hands. He took their place. When the pit was deep enough he had some tree-trunks cut and put them in as props. The stench of humid soil, of rotting leaves and stones washed by the rains pervaded his soaked drill clothing more potently than ever. At last Perken and he succeeded in dragging out the stone. It toppled over, revealing its under side swarming with gray wood-lice which had taken refuge there during the excavation.

So now they possessed the dancing-girls' heads and feet; only the bodies remained on the middle stone, which projected from the wall like an overhanging turret.

Perken picked up the sledge-hammer and set to striking at the remaining stone. He expected it to give at the first blow; but it did nothing of the kind. He continued raining blows on it, mechanically, a prey once more to furious anger. He saw his men being mowed down for lack of machine-guns, flying in panic before a line of charging elephants. As he went on hammering and his thoughts grew blurred, he was gradually possessed by the sensual thrill which comes of every long-protracted struggle. Once more his blows were uniting him with his enemy, the stone.

Suddenly he noticed that the blows were sounding differently. He caught his breath, pulled off his glare-glasses. At first he had only a confused impression of a medley of blues and greens; then, as he blinked, one thing alone filled the whole field of his vision. The stone had split! Sunlight sparkled on the break; the sculptured frontage had split off clean and was lying on the ground, like a newly severed head.

He breathed again, a slow, deep breath. Claude, too, had a feeling of vast relief. Had he been weaker he would have wept. The world flowed back into him as into a man who has just escaped from drowning. The insensate gratitude he had felt on seeing the first sculptured figure welled up in him anew. Thanks to the fallen stone, he was suddenly in harmony with the forest and the temple. He pictured the three stones as they had been, one above the other; the two dancing-girls were some of the purest work he had ever seen. Well, the next thing was to load them on to the carts. . . . But he could not get his thoughts off the stones; had he been asleep he would surely have wakened, did anyone lay hands on them. The natives had begun to roll the three blocks, one after the other, along the track they had cleared. Watching his hard-won prize, and listening to the gentle thudding of the stones as they rolled over and flattened out the cane-stems, Claude caught himself counting the thuds, as a miser counts his gold.

The natives halted when they reached the great mound of débris by the gate. The oxen were not lowing, but Claude could hear them paw the ground. Perken had two more tree-trunks cut down; then he slipped ropes round one of the stones and lashed it to the trunk. Six of the natives put their shoulders under it. But the weight proved too much for them. Claude replaced two of them by the boy and himself.

"Hoist!"

The six straightened themselves up, all together this time, slowly, in a dead silence.

Just then there was the crisp sound of a breaking twig, followed by more noises of the same kind; the noises seemed to be approaching. Claude halted and tried to plumb the depths of the forest, but, as usual, he could make out nothing. Perhaps some inquisitive native from the last village was spying on them. Or was it Svay? Claude made a sign to Perken, who came and took his place under the tree-trunk. Drawing his revolver, he went in the direction the sounds had come from. The natives who had heard the noise made by his revolver as he took it from the holster and then, more faintly, the click of the release safety-catch, looked on, puzzled and uneasy. Withdrawing his hands from the trunk, Perken propped it on his shoulder so as to be free to draw his revolver. Meanwhile Claude had gone some way into the jungle, but he could only see a maze of glimmering shadows spangled here and there by spiders' webs. Anyhow it was ridiculous to think of tracking down a native familiar with the forest. Perken had not moved. Then, a couple of yards over Claude's head, the branches dipped and swung up again, launching gray balls that shot up through the air, to land on other branches, which sagged beneath their impact. The gray balls were monkeys. Claude turned round, expecting a chorus of laughter. But the natives did not laugh. Claude walked back to them.

"It's only monkeys!"

"Not *only* monkeys," Perken replied. "Monkeys don't make branches break."

Claude put his revolver back in the holster; a futile gesture in the vast silence which had resumed its sway over all the teeming life that festered in the foul decomposition of the forest. He went back to his place amongst the natives holding up the tree-trunk. In a few minutes the mound of rubble was surmounted. He told the men to bring their carts as near as possible; they came so close that Perken had to ask them to move back a little so as to give more room for handling the stones. Intent on their little oxen, the cartmen stared at the stones lashed round with ropes, with blank indifference.

Claude was the last to move. The covered carts plunged leisurely into the leafage, pitching like boats in a rough sea. At each revolution of the wheels the axles creaked, and at regular intervals there came a bump as if each pair of wheels in turn was striking against a concealed root. Claude hardly glanced back at the open trail their passage left behind them in the jungle growth, or at the fallen canes some of which, only half crushed, were slowly swinging up again. Nor did he notice the bright scar on the wall whence they had cut the stone, lit by the ray of sunlight that had flashed on the claw-hammer at the crucial moment. He felt his muscles going limp, and to his fever and the heat was added now a sense of utter physical exhaustion. And yet, he realized, the spell of the forest, of its lianas and the spongy leaves, was weakening; against their sorcery the stones he had secured served as a counter-charm. The forest could no longer dominate his thoughts, which moved lethargically to the slow rhythm of the heavy-laden carts forging ahead. The heavy load gave a new stridency to their creaking axles as they lumbered on towards the mountains. Some red ants fell on to his sleeve; he shook them off, leapt on his pony and caught up the carts. As soon as there was room enough to do so he rode past them all, one by one. As usual, he noticed, the cartmen looked half asleep.

3

Night came at last, marking another stage of their long trek towards the mountains. The oxen were un-yoked and the stones stowed away, like new-bought acquisitions slipped into a pocket, under the rest-house roof. His limbs relaxed, as after a warm bath, Claude sauntered to and fro between the stilt-like piles on which the mat-huts stood. Before the primitive clay Buddhas, each sheltered by a little roof of thatch, joss-sticks were smoldering, rose-pink pin-heads flecking the flood of moonlight. A shadow crept across the ground towards Claude's feet and soundlessly drew up alongside his. Looking round, he saw the boy had come up from behind him, and was standing there sharply silhouetted against a mass

115

of plantain leaves that sparkled with a phosphorescent sheen.

"Master. Svay gone."

"Sure?"

"Sure."

"A good riddance!"

The bare-footed boy vanished silently away as though he had dissolved into the greenish haze that filled the clearing. "A smart chap, that boy of mine," Claude thought. . . . It certainly looked as if Svay were acting under orders. Well, he had no objection to a straight fight with an avowed enemy; indeed the prospect of an open conflict whetted his determination.

In the rest-house he found Perken already asleep, lying on his face, his hands half-clenched. Claude, too, lay down—but not to sleep. He could not quell the feverish excitement his new-won possession had aroused in him. In the brilliant moonlight the voices of the natives seemed to carry further and more clearly, but, as night advanced, they grew silent one by one. All he now heard was the drone of a storyteller and, at times, a burst of voices from the headman's hut. Then all the sounds died out into the vast silence of the tropical night, still as the moon-steeped air, and broken only by the distant crowing of a jungle-cock, a lonely sound lost in the frozen calm of some dead planet.

Towards midnight he was roused by a curious noise, so very faint he was surprised it should have wakened him; it sounded as if leafy branches were being trailed along the ground. His first glance went to the stones, which had been placed, under his orders, between his camp-bed and Perken's. Dacoits, planning a raid on the village, would certainly not have chosen a moment when white men were there. As, little by little, he became fully awake, his energy came back. He took a few steps in front of the rest-house; nothing was visible but the sleeping village and its long blue shadows. After he had gone back to bed he continued listening intently for an hour or so; the air seemed quivering like a lake under the soft night-wind. The only sound of life he heard was the lowing of sleepy cattle. Slowly the intervals of utter silence lengthened, and he fell asleep again.

When he awoke at sunrise a wave of joy, greater than any he had ever known, flooded his thoughts. The steadfast purpose which for so many months had urged him on towards an uncertain goal had justified itself. He jumped down from the flooring of the rest-house without using the steps, and hastened towards the water-bucket near which his boy was standing, striped like a convict by shadows of the overhanging branches.

"Master," the boy whispered in his ear. "No way getting carts in village."

Some defensive instinct all but prompted Claude to have the words repeated to him, but he realized at once it would have served no purpose.

"Where have they taken the carts?" he asked.

"To jungle, sure. Gone 'way last night."

"Svay's work."

"No one else can doing it."

No prospect of trans-shipping, then; and no carts meant—no stones. He remembered the noise of trailing branches he had heard.

"And our own carts?" he asked. "What about them?"

"Drivers sure not wanting go further. Shall I asking?"

Claude ran back to the rest-house and woke Perken, who smiled when his eyes fell on the stones.

"Svay cleared off last night with the villagers' carts and all the drivers. So we can't trans-ship our stones. And, of course, the cartmen who came with us will insist on going back to their village. . . . Look here, for goodness' sake, wake up!"

Perken plunged his head into the water. Monkeys were chattering in the distance. He dried his face and returned to Claude who was sitting on the bed and seemed to be working out a sum on his fingers.

"Solution number one. We can go and hunt up the fellows who've cleared off."

"Nothing doing."

"Nothing like a bucket of water for clearing one's ideas, eh? Or we might force our own cartmen to carry on."

"No. . . . Well, with a hostage, possibly."

118

"What d'you mean?"

"I mean, we can keep one of them under . . . observation, and threaten to shoot him if the others let us down."

Xa came back, carrying two topees, for the sun was striking on their heads. His face wore the look of a prematurely aged child, serious beyond his years.

"I been seeing, master. Our cartmen, too, gone 'way."

"What's that?"

"I say they not gone because I seeing carts. Our carts not gone; only village carts gone. But all cartmen, they gone 'way."

Claude walked to the hut behind which the carts had been unloaded on the previous evening when they had come from the temple; the carts were still there and, tethered near them, the little bullocks. Perhaps Svay had been afraid of waking the white men if he had the carts driven away from so near the rest-house.

"Xa, do you know how to drive cart?"

"Sure, master."

Except for some women the village was deserted. Should they leave the ponies behind and drive the carts themselves? It was only a matter of letting the other bullocks follow the leading cart, which Xa, of course, would drive. They had none too many carts; only three, all told. But, if the ponies were left behind, how in case of an attack could they hope to defend themselves? Nothing could be done from a bullock-cart. Claude needed all the fanatical determination which his resolve to carry on and to advance despite the jungle's hostility, and men's as well, inspired in him, in order to fight down a sense of enfeeblement, a feeling they had been deserted and the forest once again was beginning to assert its domination.

"Xa!" Perken shouted. "What's become of the guide?"

"He cleared off, master."

So now they had no guide! Unaided, they must cross the mountains; strike the pass, unaided. And in the frontier villages, peopled by fever-stricken natives, where at nightfall the air hummed with mosquitoes thick as motes in sunlight, they would have to find new cartmen . . . push on, somehow.

"We have the compass," Claude remarked, "and Xa. There are so few tracks that we're sure to be able to spot the right ones."

"If you're quite determined to end up as a little heap of garbage alive with maggots, your idea strikes me as sound enough. . . . Put your hat on your head, instead of holding it like that. The sun's getting high."

"Anyhow let's try," Claude all but answered. Yet, despite his eagerness to quit this village whose inhabitants had fled as if before an invading army, and the clearing ringed by giant tree-trunks which in the level light of morning loomed huger still, he hesitated. That, somehow or other, he would push on was a foregone conclusion—but how?

"Plenty of the natives," Perken went on, "in this part of the country know the road leading to the mountains. I'll go along with Xa to that little village without a rest-house which we passed on our way here; Takay, the name was. There's no hope of getting cartmen, but I'll bring back a guide. I don't think Svay's been there."

While he spoke the boy was saddling the ponies.

Swaying to the jerky trot of their mounts, Perken and the boy vanished down a leafy tunnel, like miners entering an adit; here and there a sudden shaft of light struck down through the close-woven roof, changing their forms from black to green. "If they unearth a guide at once," Claude thought, "and speed him up, they'll be back by noon. *If* they find one!" For might not Svay have made the villagers decamp from Takay, too?

The ladders had been drawn up into the huts. In the tremulous air, every outline was losing its fixity, caught in the shimmering mirage that ushers in the blaze of noon. Claude lay down on the camp-bed, his chin between his hands. A guide . . . to lead them to the mountains. Would they find him? On all sides of the clearing, around this zone of living light and habitations built by men, stretched far and wide the jungle, motionless yet never quite at rest. Traversed by slow vibrations the light fell on its surface, breaking into ripples like shot silk. Supple and soft as silk the warm waves lapped his sweating skin till he grew dazed with sunlight and sank into a daydream clouded with darker intervals of sleep.

He was awakened by a rapid thudding, the sound of horse-hooves in the far distance. Eleven o'clock. "That guide must be a champion sprinter," he murmured to himself. He held his breath, intently listening, frowning a little. The sound rose from the soil; from the depths of the jungle the ponies were galloping towards him. But surely, after two hours' march, a man couldn't keep up with ponies at the gallop. Why were they hurrying back like that? he wondered. He tried to catch a sound of footsteps, but could only hear the heavy silence of the clearing, a thin hum of insects close to the ground, and, far away, the brisk *staccato* of the ponies' iron-shod feet.

He ran out on to the road. The drumming grew nearer and at last he saw two shadowy forms bobbing up and down as they galloped towards him. Then, as they crossed a shaft of light, he clearly saw them bending over their ponies' necks, their sun-helmets set back on their heads. No runner between them. . . . He had a fleeting impression, not of catastrophe, but of slow, nauseous, ineluctable decay. The riders had grown shadow-like again. Suddenly, as they entered another column of light, they became clearly visible. Claude noticed that Xa was leaning forward more than ever and that two pale patches,

122

a man's hands, hung on his shoulders; someone was riding pillion behind him.

"Well?"

"Things look pretty foul!" Perken replied as he jumped down from his pony.

"Svay . . . ?"

"Does his job well. He's been there, called away all the men who know the passes, and is taking them down south."

"Who's that fellow there?"

"He knows the road to the Moi villages."

"What are the tribes on the way?"

"Ke-Diengs—they belong to the Stieng group. Anyhow, there's nothing else for it."

"Nothing, you mean, except moving into the unpacified tract at once."

"Yes. If we follow the Way, we have three kinds of country before us; an unknown region, an administered tract and the unpacified tract. In the administered area, God only knows what tricks your French administration will be up to."

"Yes, Ramèges will see red when he hears we've made a find."

"That means—we must give up the idea of making the big pass and cross directly into the unpacified area. The guide I've brought knows the paths leading to the first Stieng village—the one where the bartering takes place—and the way on from there into Siam, over the smaller passes."

"Then we strike due west, I suppose?"

"Yes."

"But, these Stiengs you mentioned—you don't know anything about them?"

"We've got no choice. We're bound to make for the region where Grabot's likely to be found. All the guide can say is that there's a white man somewhere in those parts. Anyhow he knows the Stieng dialect, that's something. Once we reach the village we'll get another guide; we shall have to make a formal application to the local headman to let us through, and we'll see what sort of answer they give. I've still two thermos flasks full of alcohol, as well as the glass beads—quite enough to pay our right of way. I don't know the tribe myself, but I expect they'll know who I am. If Grabot doesn't want us to come where he is, he'll send a guide to side-track us, I expect."

"Are you sure they'll let us through?"

"We've got to try, anyhow. As we shall have to cross the unpacified tracts in any case, why not enter them at once? The guide tells me they're a fighting race, but they'll stand by an oath taken on rice-spirit."

The Cambodian, a short, sturdy fellow, hook-nosed like the local Buddhas, had just alighted from the horse, and stood there waiting, with folded hands. Near by someone was honing a wood-knife —preparatory to splitting coconuts, perhaps. Xa pricked up his ears. Abruptly the noise ceased; through chinks in the mat-walls the village women

124

were observing the white men mistrustfully, with restless, curious eyes.

"What brought Grabot to these parts?" Claude asked.

"Eroticism, principally—though the women here are a damned sight uglier than those in Laos; power means for him, I should say . . . the possibility of abusing it."

"Has he brains?"

Perken began laughing, but suddenly stopped short, as if the sound of his own laughter took him by surprise.

"When you know the man," he replied, "the question sounds ridiculous, and yet . . . He's never given a thought to anything except himself, or, more exactly, the side of his character which makes him a man apart; he's set on it as other men are set on gambling or authority. Not much of a personality, perhaps, but—there's something in him, that's sure. It's his courage that distinguishes him. He's far more isolated than you or I from other men, because he has no hope at all, not the least glimmer of hope —only his courage—and because a man's imagination, however blunted, serves as a link between him and the outside world. I remember something he said to me once, speaking of the 'others'—meaning people for whom men of his kind simply don't exist —the law-abiding sort, the 'slave-men.' 'It's only through their pleasures you can get at them; one would need to invent something on the lines of syphilis.' When he was drafted into a penal battalion he was as keen as mustard about his fellow-soldiers, whom he'd never met before. On the voyage out a canvas partition separated the 'rookies' from the habituals and recaptured runaways. There were some holes in the canvas. Grabot put his eye to one of them, but recoiled at once; something had made a jab at it—an extended finger with a gnawed but pointed nail, which might easily have gouged his eye out. Yes, Grabot's a man who's absolutely *alone,* and, like all lonely men, he needs something to make up for his loneliness; in his case it's courage. I wish I could make it clear somehow. . . ." He groped amongst his memories.

If, Claude reflected, all he's been saying is correct, that man must have some solid, indisputable ground for living, something that enables him to admire himself. . . .

A murmur of insects' wings droned on the tranquil air. Leisurely a black pig advanced towards them, as if it were in sole possession of the silent village.

"This," Perken continued, "is more or less how he put it. 'Either you damn well care, or you don't, about getting yourself done in. I'm playing a poker game all by myself—see?—that the other fellows won't cut into; the mere idea of breaking their precious necks sets 'em jittering. Not me. A blasted good thing it'll be, in fact it's about the only thing on earth I can make a good, clean job of. And, as I don't give a hoot whether I croak or not—what's more, I rather like the idea of it—things can go as they damn well choose. If they go badly, they can't go any further than the muzzle of my revolver. See? I got my way out ready.' And he's the genuine article, a really brave man. He knows he's short on brains, and feels an outsider when he strikes the towns; so he makes up for it by living with his courage—it's wife and family to him. He finds the same pleasure that we all do in risking our lives, but for him the pleasure's all the keener because it's more essential to him. And he's capable of more than merely taking risks; he has an instinct for a sort of—what shall I call it?—a brutal heroism; primitive, I grant you, but decidedly out of the common. I told you the way he lost his eye, didn't I? And then, going away like that, all by himself, into these parts—well, it needs some pluck, you know. You've heard of the sting of the black scorpion? No? Well I know what the gouges feel like; the scorpion hurts even worse, and that's saying quite a lot. Just because he felt a violent nervous repulsion the first time he saw one of the brutes, he deliberately got himself bitten. Once a man decides to cut himself off completely—*completely*, mind you—from his fellow men, he's always bound to inflict terrible sufferings on himself, simply to prove his strength. Behind it all there's a sort of rugged pride which life, and a series of hard knocks, have hammered more or less into shape. Helping a pal who'd got into some damn-fool scrape or other, he was very nearly eaten alive by red ants; but that's not quite so horrible as it sounds, however, when you remember his ideas about using his revolver."

"You don't think one can *always* kill oneself?"

"Quite possibly it's no harder to die for oneself— in one's own interest, I mean—than to live for one-self; but I'm not so sure about it. Obviously it's up to a man to kill himself when he feels he's wearing out, but that's the very time when he starts loving life again. Still, Grabot thinks it can be done—so much the better for him!"

"Suppose he's dead?"

(The village huts seemed more and more hermet-ically closed.)

"They'd have sold his European kit and the guide would know about it, and so would all the other na-tives in the barter-village. I've questioned him; nothing's been sold. We'll have to make the official demand to the headman to let us through, in any case. . . ." He glanced round the village. "Women, only women here! A village given up to the women —doesn't it affect you at all, this atmosphere with-out a hint of maleness in it, all these women, the drowsy air, reeking of sex. . . ."

"Better hold up your thrills for further on! It's time to be moving now."

The boy piled their camp-kit into a cart and yoked the oxen. Each cart in turn halted before the rest-house; the stones were lifted down gingerly in Claude's camp-bed. At last the carts lumbered off, the guide driving the foremost cart, Xa the next. Sitting in the third cart, Claude made little attempt to drive his oxen, letting them amble on after the others. Perken, on horseback, brought up the rear. The boy had untethered Claude's pony and it followed them slowly, its nose close to the ground. Its docility gave Perken an idea. "Better keep that pony with us," he murmured, and attached its bridle to the cart in front of him. Just as a bend of the road was taking them out of sight of the village, he glanced back; some wattles had been let down, and the women were peering after them with puzzled, curious eyes.

Part Three

1

In the midst of these half-savage tribes which had
successfully withstood inclusion in a protectorate, life
was no less uncertain, no less precarious than in the
forest. In the village where the bartering took
place, a village even more dilapidated than the temples, what few Cambodians there were seemed terror-
stricken, and parried every question about the other
villages, about the tribal chiefs, about Grabot. Perken's name, however, was not unknown to them, or
so it seemed. They had not a trace of the sensual,
easy-going temperament of the Laos and Lower Cambodians. Here were real savages; one smelled their
meaty smell. At last the messengers reported that,
in return for two bottles of European spirit, the

133

party would be permitted to travel through the tribe's territory and be given a guide. They were unable to discover from whom the permit came. But, as they moved up-country to the Stieng headquarters, a far more pressing problem forced itself upon their minds. Claude was brought up sharply by a blow on the arm from Perken.

"Look down. Don't move."

Less than three inches from his right foot two extremely sharp splinters of bamboo protruded from the ground, like the prongs of a fork. Perken pointed again.

"What else?" Claude asked.

Perken's only answer was a low whistle. Then he flung his cigarette in front of him. Through the green air, turbid with the shadows of impending night, it described a fiery red parabola, and fell on to the soft mold lining the side of the cart-track. Near the place where it had fallen Claude saw two more bamboo spikes.

"What gadgets are those?"

"War-spikes."

Claude glanced at the Moi tribesman who was waiting for them—they had changed guides at the village—leaning on his cross-bow.

"That fellow should have warned us, shouldn't he?" Claude asked.

"I don't like the look of things at all."

They shuffled along the track, hardly daring to

lift their feet from the ground, following the yellow object in front of them—their guide. His sarong was incredibly filthy; it seemed mottled with blood. Claude felt that the man was neither wholly human nor altogether bestial. Each time he had to lift his foot—to cross a tree-trunk or a root—he felt the sinews of his leg contract, dreading to take an over-hasty step. He groped his way ahead like a blind man, his muscles shrinking from the hidden dangers of the way. Try as he might to see, his eyes were practically useless; his sense of smell replaced them and he sniffed uneasily the gusts of tepid air, reeking with heavy fumes of mold. How could he see the spikes, if rotting leaves all but covered up the track? He was helpless as a slave; his legs seemed shackled. For all his efforts to master a desire to tread with extreme circumspection, the spasms in his calves were more imperious than his will.

"What about the bullocks, Perken? Supposing one of them's brought down?"

"There's not much danger of that. They feel the spikes much sooner than we can."

He thought of riding in one of the carts behind, of which Xa was the only driver. But, if he did so, he would be incapable of resisting an attack.

They crossed the dry bed of a stream. The crossing was a welcome respite; in that pebbly surface, any-how, nothing could lurk hidden. A few yards away they saw three Mois standing on a bank of clayey soil, one above the other, staring at them with blank, inhuman fixity; their eyes seemed dead and stony, facets of the universal silence.

"If things turn out badly," Perken observed, "some of these blighters will be taking us in the rear."

The eyes of the savages followed their retreat, impassive as before. Only one of them had a cross-bow. The track was getting less dark; the trees did not stand quite so thickly together. They were still obliged to walk warily, but the obsession of the war-spikes was losing its hold on them. At last a glade, open to the declining sun, showed up in front.

The guide halted. Some thin strands of rattan were stretched neck-high across the track, covered with tiny thorns which glistened in the sun and tapered off into invisibility. The guide unfastened the strands. Claude had failed to notice them. "If," he said to himself, "we land in a mess, it'll be none too easy getting away."

When they had passed, the Moi carefully replaced the saw-like strands as he had found them.

No track was visible across the glade. Still one, at least, must lead away from it, continuing the track which had brought them there. For all its air of peacefulness, there was something sinister about the glade, their camping-place for the coming night. Half of it was already submerged in darkness, and the other half lit only by the bright yellow glow which precedes the nightfall. No palm-trees were to be seen; Asia was manifest only in the heat, in the

huge bulk of some red tree-trunks, and in the brooding silence, which the hum of myriads of insects and,
now and then, the lone cry of a bird swooping down
on a lofty branch, seemed to render vaster still, still
more impressive. Like stagnant water the heavy silence closed down on all these vagrant sounds, while
high aloft the bough swayed gently, gently swaying
in the dusk. Beyond the trackless masses of vegetation cataracting down steep declivities that fell away
into the evening mist, the mountains stood out
sharply against the dying sky. The Mois, like the
woodworms that infest the giant trees, fought with
small but deadly weapons. In the great hush of the
forest their furtive methods, their inexplicable wariness, seemed all the more ominous. They had only
to deal with three men without an escort, led by a
guide whom the tribesmen had provided of their
own accord; what possible need was there for those
spikes or rattan strands? Why should the glade have
been defended in this manner? "Does it mean that
Grabot is sparing no pains to keep his liberty of action?" Claude asked himself. And, as though the very
rarity of thoughts in this oasis of the forest had made
Claude's silent question audible, Perken answered it.

"I'm convinced that he isn't alone."

"What do you mean?"

"Not the only *chief*. Or else it would mean that
he's gone native, through and through. . . ."

He paused. The implications of his words seemed
to permeate the dreaming forest, to find their illus-

tration in the squatting guide busily scratching a knee blotched by the scabs of some foul skin-disease.

". . . that he has become another man, in fact," Perken concluded.

Once more they had come up against the unknown. Their venture was urging them towards this man as it had led them along the invisible alignment of the Royal Way. And now he, too, stood between them and their appointed destiny. Still, he had granted them the right of way. . . .

The photographs which Perken had brought from Bangkok loomed as vividly in Claude's remembrance as if a fixed idea had limned them there. He saw a sturdy, jovial, one-eyed adventurer who roamed the jungle and haunted the Chinese bars of Siam, his topee on the back of his head, his mouth agape and eyelids puckered with gargantuan laughter. Claude had seen faces in which, across the grossness of maturity, there somehow showed a hint of childish candor. It showed itself in a laugh, in the way the eyes grew rounded with surprise, in carefree gestures. Thus he could picture Grabot slamming a topee down over the ears of a pal, or of an enemy. But, in these primitive surroundings, how much of the townsman would have survived? As Perken said, he well might have "gone native."

Claude went to look for the guide. He found him crooning a native chant, for the benefit of Xa alone, beside the motionless oxen. The fires they had kindled for the night were making little explosive noises not far from the camp-beds which had been set up under mosquito-nets. The tents had not been pitched, on account of the heat.

"Better take down the mosquito-nets," Perken said. "It's bad enough knowing that blasted fire will keep us in full view. At least let's try to get a sight of any-one attacking us."

The glade was wide, and an assailant would have to cross a patch of open ground.

"If anything happens," Perken continued, "the one who's on watch shoots down the guide; then we'll slip behind that bush there on the right, so as to get out of the light of the fire."

"But, even if we beat them off, how can we carry on without a guide?"

Whatever might be threatening them seemed to depend on Grabot; he held the master cards that would decide their fate.

"Have you any idea what his game can be?" Claude asked.

"Grabot's?"

"Obviously."

"Now that we're so close to him, so near what we've been expecting of him, I've almost lost faith in my theories. . . ."

The fire went on sputtering, but the flames rose straight and bright. They were almost pink, and lit up only the leaping spirals of their own smoke. The glow the fire cast on the walls of leafage all around was hardly distinguishable from the sky. Now that

Perken was confronted with the last move of the game on which he had staked so much, he realized he did not know his man.

"After all the spikes we've seen, do you still suppose he means to let us through?"

"If he's on his own, yes."

"And you're sure he has no notion of the value of our stones?"

Perken shrugged his shoulders.

"That's quite beyond him," he replied. "Why, I myself . . ."

"But, if he's not on his own, mayn't there be someone with him who knows?"

"Well, it certainly isn't a white man. . . . Anyhow, fellows who have nerve enough to come up into these parts usually stand by each other. What's more, I've done Grabot a good turn or two." He paused, lost in thought, his eyes fixed on the grass beside his feet. "I'd like to know what it can be that he's trying to ward off," he said at last. "It's with his early dreams, his sense of degradation that a man keeps his passions alive."

"It depends on what his passions are."

"I told you of a fellow who used to get women at Bangkok to tie him up naked. That was Grabot. After all it isn't so very much sillier than to propose to sleep and live—to live!—with another human creature. But he feels damnably humiliated by it."

"Because other people know?"

140

"Nobody knows about it. Because of himself, because he does it. So he tries *to make up for it*. That, I imagine, is the chief reason that brought him here. Courage atones for a great deal. And then—don't all the little things we are ashamed of seem insignificant beside all this?"

As if the sweep of an arm were utterly inadequate to indicate the majesty about them, he contented himself with a quick jerk of his chin towards the clearing and the far mountains dissolving into darkness. Now the tall barrier of trees was drenched in shadow and above the great primeval forest brooding round them a host of stars outshone their leaping fire; the slow, tremendous progress of the night overwhelmed Claude with a sense of supreme loneliness, making him feel once more a hunted thing at bay. And in the lambent darkness he discerned an ineluctable indifference, an immanence of death.

"Yes, I can understand he doesn't care a damn about dying."

"That's not it. It's not death that he doesn't fear—death is something quite outside his range. It's this; he's not afraid of being killed. . . . Of course there's nothing much in that—not being afraid of getting a bullet in one's head." He lowered his voice. "But, if the bullet gets you in the belly, it's less agreeable. A long drawn out business; pretty beastly. You know as well as I do that life is meaningless; when a man lives alone he can't help brooding over the problem of his destiny. And death is always there, you see, ahead of him, like . . . like a standing proof of the futility of life."

"For each of us."

"For nobody! It exists for nobody. Very few of us could go on living if . . . But everyone bears in mind the fact that—how'm I to make you see what I'm driving at?—that he may be killed. That's what I mean. To be killed—that's of no importance. But death, death is different; it's the exact opposite, in fact. You're too young, of course. . . . I realized it the first time I saw a woman growing old, a woman whom . . . well, a woman I knew. (But I've told you about Sarah, haven't I?) Then, too, as if that warning wasn't enough, there was that time—the first time—when I found that I was impotent." The words forced their way out painfully; to rise to the surface they had to wrench their way through a mesh of strangling roots. "No," Perken continued, "I never got that feeling from the sight of a dead body. To grow old, that's it—to peter out. Especially when one's cut off from others. A death-in-life. What weighs on me is—how shall I put it?—my human lot, my limitations; that I must grow old, and time, that loathsome thing, spread through me like a cancer, inevitably. Time—there you have it! D'you see all those damn-fool insects making for our lamp, obeying the call of the light? The termites, too, obey the law of the anthill. I . . . *I will not obey*."

The forest had awakened with the great stir of

nightfall; the wild life of the earth rose with the darkness. Claude felt incapable of putting further questions. The words formed in his mind passed over Perken's as above a subterranean river. By all the immensity of the forest such a man was sundered from those to whom reason and truth are real; could he appeal to any human aid in fighting down the phantoms massed around him in the gloom? He had just drawn his revolver; a glint of light flickered along the barrel.

"My whole life depends on how I regard the act of pressing this trigger when I put the barrel between my lips. The point is: do I then believe I am destroying myself, or that I am taking a definite step forward? Life is so much raw material; what is one making of it?—that's the question. It's true one never can make anything of it, really; still there are several methods of making nothing of it. And, in order to live one's life *according to plan,* one must have a short way with life's threats, the threat of growing old, of wearing out, and so forth. So a revolver is an excellent life-insurance, for it's easy enough to kill oneself when death is a means. . . . That's where Grabot's strength lies."

The last glow had left the sky. All Asia had passed into the night, the dark dominion of solitude and silence. Above the faint crackling of the fire, they could hear the voices of the two natives, monotonous and shrill, but devoid of resonance—imprisoned voices. Near at hand the steady tick of an alarm-clock meted out the silence of the jungle, and, more than the campfire, more even than the voices, its punctual tick brought Claude back to the world of living men. Here, anyhow, was something precise and clear-cut, functioning with the stolid perseverance of every reliable machine. His thoughts rose to the plane of full awareness, but enriched by all that they had drawn from the depths whence they emerged, and still in thrall to the elemental influences of darkness and the sun-scorched earth. It was as if all things, even the earth itself, were seeking to convince him of the futility of human life.

"And the *other* death, the death that is within us . . . ?"

"To live on in defiance of all that"—Perken's eyes indicated the tremendous menace of the night—"can you realize what that means? To live defying death is the same thing. It seems to me sometimes that I am staking myself, all that I am, on a single moment—my last. And, very likely, it will come quite soon; some more or less filthy arrow will settle the business, once for all."

"One doesn't choose one's death."

"No doubt. And, having waived my choice of death, I've had to choose my life."

The red glint on his shoulder flickered; he had made an unseen gesture in the darkness. A puny gesture, as puny as the little human speck whose feet were hidden in shadow, whose fitful voice floated up into the starry depths. A man's voice, lonely and

144

remote, poised between the shining sky, and death, and darkness; yet in it there was something so inhuman that Claude felt as isolated from it as he would have been by incipient madness.

"Then you want to die," Claude asked, "with an intense awareness of death, and yet without . . . flinching?"

"I've been very near death. And you can't imagine the wild elation of those moments—it's the sudden glimpse of the absurdity of life that brings it—when one meets death face to face, naked"—he made a gesture as of tearing off a woman's garments—"stark naked suddenly. . . ."

Keeping his eyes fixed on the glittering sky, Claude answered:

"Nearly everyone bungles his death, one way or other."

"I spend my life with death in view. But I know what you mean—for you, too, are afraid—and it's true enough. Very likely when my time comes I'll fail to rise to the occasion. . . . So much the worse! And, anyhow, there's something satisfactory in the mere thought that life is being annihilated."

"You've never thought seriously of killing yourself?"

"When I think about my death it's with a view to living—not to dying."

There could be no mistaking the tension in his voice; it expressed a bitter joy, emptied of every hope, like wave-worn jetsam drawn up from sea-depths deep as the dark night around them.

2

They had set out at dawn, and several hours' march lay behind them; the war-spikes were fewer here, but the leeches pestilent as ever. Now and again a loud chattering of monkeys shrilled down the valley, rippling like aërial laughter above the dull thuds of the cart-wheels jolting over hidden tree-stumps.

At the end of the cart-track, blurred like a landscape seen through misted field-glasses, the Stieng village straggled across an open glade. In its stockaded walls Claude saw the menace of an unknown weapon; now that the carts were near it, the wooden rampart blotted out the forest, and the impression of vicious force it gave was intensified by the only objects visible above it: a tall tomb with fetishes

146

composed of feathers, and a huge gaur's skull. Then
molten light of noon shimmered on its horns; it
seemed as if the forest, beating a retreat behind the
high stockade, had left as only token of its presence
these curious trophies poised in mid-air against the
leafless sky. The guide unfastened some more rattan
strands and, when the carts had passed, replaced
them.

The gate was ajar. They entered the village. A
Moi sentry posted at the gate pushed it to behind
them with the butt end of a gun.

"At last!" Claude exclaimed. "That means Grabot's somewhere here."

Perken had time to notice that the hammer of the
gun was up before the rattle of the closing gate
urged him forward. On their right a jumble of squat
huts sprawled on the soil like jungle beasts, and some
small pariah dogs, posted on a rubbish-heap, barked
at the white men. From the huts men and women
peered at them suspiciously over the edges of low
bamboo wattles.

The guide led them to a hut that was somewhat
higher than the rest; it stood in an open space beside
the pole that bore the skull of the wild ox. No less
than the huge horns pointing skywards like uplifted
arms, the high hut seemed to dominate the peopled
solitude. That, Claude reflected, must be the chief's
house, or a tribal headquarters; Grabot, perhaps,
was living beneath that palm-thatched roof, under
the spreading horns. If they had reached this place

147

in safety, it was Grabot's doing. Following the guide, they climbed the ladder, entered the hut and squatted down.

Their eyes were not yet used to the dim light, but they realized at once that no white man was present. Perken rose, moved a few steps forward and squatted down again, turning a little to one side—a posture of respect, it seemed; Claude followed his example. Some dozen warriors took their stand at the far end of the hut—till now they had been following the newcomers—each of them armed with the short Stieng sword, a cross between the native wood-knife and a saber. One of them began to scratch his head; Perken heard the rasping nails before he saw the man.

"Slip your safety-catch," he whispered hurriedly.

Obviously he could not be referring to the Colt which Claude carried on his belt. Then he heard a faint click and saw Perken take from his pocket a handful of glass trinkets. He slipped back the safety-catch of the little Browning in his pocket—very slowly, so as to make the least noise possible—and produced some bright blue beads. Perken had already held out his hand to take them; now he made over the beads and trinkets, saying some words in Siamese which the guide translated.

"Look, Claude!" he whispered. "Above the head of the old fellow who seems to be the chief." Something loomed white amongst the shadows: a European's jacket. "Grabot must be somewhere about."

The old chief grinned, his lips drawn tight over his gums. Then he raised two fingers.

"They're going to bring the jar—for the oath ceremony, you know."

A triangular shaft of light fell from the roof, slashing the old chief's body from shoulder to hip; it left his eunuch-like head in semi-darkness, but showed up his collar-bone and ribs in bright relief. Now his eyes wandered from the white men to the shadow of the gaur's skull splayed flat before his feet; to the least detail its form lay shadow-stenciled on the floor, only the horns were tangled by the perspective. The shadow began to flicker as if a sudden thud they had just heard had jogged it. A jar rose into view at the top of the ladder, with a reed projecting from its neck; two hands clasped it on either side, the fingers straight and lying flat against the sides in ritual immobility, like sculptured handles. Proffered between the two uplifted wrists, it looked like an oblation to the quivering shadow, a sacrament of peace. Some more soft thuds followed; the man who bore the jar, after touching the totem-pole, was feeling for the rungs of the ladder. At last he loomed up in the doorway, clad in a tattered blue Cambodian costume. (Even the Moi chief wore only a loin-cloth.) Slowly, holding himself erect, he took some steps forward, then lowered the jar to the floor with extraordinary circumspection. Claude felt Xa's fingers gripping his knee.

"What's the matter?"

The boy put a question in the Cambodian tongue; the bearer of the jar turned towards him, then swung round sharply towards the chief. Xa's fingers were digging into Claude's skin.

"Him! Master see him?" the boy exclaimed.

Claude suddenly realized that the man was blind —but there was something more than that.

"*Kmer-mieng!*" Xa cried to Perken. "*Kmer-mieng!*"

Perken translated the words for Claude. "It's a Cambodian slave."

The man sank out of sight again below the floor and made his way towards the huts. Claude strained his ears to catch another thud, half expecting the slave to jolt the totem-pole a second time as he made off. But all the rapt attention of the men assembled in the hut, the very silence brooding in the air, seemed centering round the chief's uplifted hand, poised solemnly above the jar. He lowered his head and sniffed the fumes of alcohol through the hollow reed. Then he passed it to Perken and, after him, to Claude, who partook of it without a qualm, for apprehension ousted his disgust. The restless flicker of Perken's eyes, as he strained to catch a glimpse of what was going on outside, added to his uneasiness.

"It makes things damned awkward," Perken said, "Grabot's not being here. Here we are pledging ourselves as regards the Mois, while Grabot's not com-

150

mitted himself in any way. I've faith in him, but all the same . . ."

"But the Mois—are they really pledging themselves?"

"None of them would dare to violate the rice-alcohol covenant. But if, in their eyes, Grabot's not bound in any way, heaven alone knows . . ."

He said something in Siamese, which the guide translated. The chief answered in a single sentence.

Brief though it was, the chief's reply had evidently much interest for the men assembled in the background, who had not stirred till now except to scratch themselves. Claude could make them out better now, and his eyes were drawn to the white blotches on their bodies, scabs left by some skin-disease. All were staring fixedly at the chief.

Perken translated the chief's words. "He says there isn't any white chief here." Then his eyes fell once more on the white jacket. "But I'm positive he's somewhere about."

Claude remembered the sentry's gun and he, too, gazed up at the shirt, which seemed to cast two shadows—on one side the true shadow, on the other a film of dust.

"That shirt hasn't been worn for a long time," he observed, lowering his voice as if he feared to be understood.

It struck him that dust might collect very quickly in the hut, but, looking round, he noticed that the floor was clean and so were the fetish-pillars. Of course it wasn't likely that Grabot would dress here as he did at Bangkok. Suddenly something that Perken had said to him when they were camping in the glade flashed into his mind, as if it had been hovering in the background all the time, suspended on the turbid air: "Or else he's gone native, through and through." For why should Grabot keep thus aloof, and, instead of meeting them in person, expose them to this ordeal, the bestial scrutiny of these savages?

Perken was talking to the chief again; their conversation was very brief.

"He says that he 'agrees'—which means absolutely nothing. As a matter of fact I mistrust the man. Anyhow I told him, to make things safer, that we'd be coming back this way and would bring him gongs and jars—in addition to the thermos-flasks of alcohol I shall give him now. That way he'll be more inclined to postpone murdering us till we come back. He doesn't believe me. There's something fishy about the whole business. We've simply got to get in touch with Grabot somehow. Once we've met him, he'd never dare . . ."

He rose; the palaver was ended. As he moved towards the ladder, he skirted the shadow of the skull as if he were afraid of coming in contact with it. The guide led them to an empty hut. Little by little the village was showing signs of life; the wattles had been let down and men in loin-cloths or blue rags—

the latter, slaves—were crowding round the hut they had just left, blundering to and fro, like blind men, in their suppressed excitement. Perken kept his eyes fixed on them as he walked towards the hut. One of them began to move towards the open space which the white men would have to cross. Perken suddenly stopped and took his foot in his hand as if a thorn had pricked it, leaning on Xa to keep his balance.

"When we meet that fellow, ask him which is the white man's hut," he whispered in Xa's ear. "Not a word more. Got it?"

The boy did not answer. The slave was close on them; there was no time for Perken to repeat his order, as the man was already within earshot. Had Xa understood? Yes—there was the boy talking to the slave, almost breast to breast. The slave's eyes were lowered, and he, too, spoke in undertones. Claude wondered if he fancied he was talking to another slave. In his eagerness to hear what the man had said Perken made a hasty movement towards Xa, and all but fell head foremost—he had quite forgotten he was holding his foot in his hand. The boy noticed his mishap and, though he was some little distance off, stretched out his arm. Perken gripped him by the wrist. "Well?" he asked. Xa wore the look of rather nervous acquiescence so often to be seen on the faces of natives inured to the white man's eccentricities. He was obviously taken aback by Perken's brusqueness and the way he had spoken, in a hoarse whisper—as if he feared someone might over-

153

hear and understand him, though on all the wide expanse of beaten earth nothing was visible except the slave's retreating figure and a dog slinking away towards a patch of shadow.

"Near the banana-trees."

There could be no mistaking where he meant; in the whole clearing there was only one clump of bananas—of the half wild variety—and beside them was a large hut. Claude came back to Perken; he was puzzled, but guessed more or less what Perken had been after.

"The slave says he's in that hut."

"What? . . . Grabot? Which hut?"

Perken pointed to it with a single finger, keeping his hand close to his hip, for safety's sake.

"Well? Shall we go there?"

"Wait a bit. Let's unyoke the bullocks first. Then they may think we've hit on it by chance—anyhow we must do our best to make it look like that."

They rejoined the guide. Xa began unyoking the oxen in front of the hut which the chief had allotted them.

"That'll do, Perken. Let's go now."

"All right."

Though they refrained from approaching it directly, the hut drew them towards it like a magnet. However much time they wasted discussing ways and means, the fact remained that they were in Grabot's hands and, if they were to come to an understanding with him, the sooner the better.

"Supposing he turns nasty?" Claude enquired.

"A bullet through his head. The only way out. In the jungle, in the region he controls, we'd be done for."

Easier said than done, Claude reflected. Wasn't Grabot up to all the tricks that can be played with a revolver—firing through a trouser-pocket and the like?

They had reached the hut. It had no windows, and a roughly-made wooden door, not a mat screen, closed the entrance. The bolt was shot—*outside*. Obviously, Perken concluded, there must be another door somewhere. Behind the hut a dog started barking.

"If he goes on making that infernal noise," Perken muttered, "we'll have the whole village on us!"

Drawing back the bolt, he gave the door a half-hearted tug, for he suspected it was barred on the inside as well. But the door yielded slowly, with an uneasy reluctance that matched his own; the wood had evidently warped during the monsoon rains.

There was the tinkle of a little bell. From the roof a single shaft of sunlight fell straight on to the floor, so thick with motes of dust that it seemed dark blue. Masses of shadow veered round and round, rising and falling, as if they were rotating on an axis. Then, as one of the circling shadows swung into view above the others, they saw distinctly what it was—an horizontal beam or spoke which something tied to its extremity was hauling round a capacious tub, a sort of vat. The tethered form was creeping towards them, but it grew blurred and shapeless once it had crossed the shaft of light that, streaming through the aperture, mingled their shadows on the dusty floor, their bodies vastly elongated, their limbs foreshortened. At last the whole mechanism showed up in the rectangle of light that lay in front of the doorway; it was a grindstone. The little bell stopped tinkling.

Perken had drawn back out of the light so as to get a better view, and Claude sidled after him, crabwise. He felt incapable of staying where he was or, when he moved, of shifting his eyes from the shaft of light which traversed the hut like a pillar of white stone. Perken continued to shrink away, and there was sheer terror in his movements. Claude guessed the nervous twitching of his fingers, groping for something solid, something to hold on to in a world falling in ruin about his head. He was incapable of speech, petrified with horror. There was a slave tethered to the grindstone, a slave with a bearded face. Was it a white man?

Perken shouted out some words, loudly enough to drown the barking of the dog, but so quickly that Claude failed to understand them. Breathlessly, he repeated them.

"What's happened? What's happened?"

The slave lurched forward through the shadows, his shoulders quivering with the strain; the bell rang out, once only, like a clock striking the half-hour. Suddenly the man stopped dead.

156

"Grabot?" Perken cried.

The accent of interrogation, the horror in his voice evoked no recognition in the face that turned towards them. Claude tried to see its eyes, but could only make out a beard, a nose. The man held forth his hand, the fingers opened, grasping for something; then it fell back against his thigh with a soft thud of flesh on flesh. He was tied to the beam by leather thongs. Claude wondered if he were blind, but, when he wished to question Perken, found he could not bring the word to his lips.

The soiled, scarred face had turned towards them —or was it not towards the light? Once more Claude tried to catch the man's eyes, in vain. The face was turned less towards him than to the door, so he had only a three-quarters view of it—and Perken had told him Grabot had lost an eye.

"Grabot!" Perken shouted, half hoping there would be no answer; and yet . . .

The man stammered some words in a husky, toneless voice.

"*Was?*" Perken gasped.

"But surely he didn't speak in German!" Claude exclaimed.

"No. Moi. It's I who lost. . . . What's that? What?"

The slave made as if to move towards them, but the thongs tethered him to the extremity of the shaft, and each movement he made followed the orbit of the grindstone.

"Go right round, damn it!"

No sooner had he begun moving than the two white men realized how terribly they dreaded the approach of this strange creature; it was not loathing or fear that made them shrink from him, rather a kind of atavistic terror, that dread of all sub-human things which Claude had felt when gazing at the pyre. Once more the man took two steps forward, and the bell tinkled twice; then he halted again.

"He understood—I'm sure of it," Claude whispered.

Though he had spoken in an undertone, the man had heard that, too.

"What is it?" he said at last, in French. His voice was toneless.

A kind of blank despair—like a dumb man's embarrassment—gripped Claude; the question invited so many answers. They might give their names, or say they were Frenchmen, or white men, or . . .

"The God-damned bastards!" Perken burst out. So far there had been a hint of interrogation in all that he had said, even when he had bidden the man "go round"; now his voice was thick with anger. Going up to the man, he told him his name. The man's eyelids—Claude could see them clearly now—looked like tightly stretched membranes adhering to an invisible bone, and they were wrinkled *vertically*. Claude fancied that if he could only touch the man, some means of communion might be contrived between them. Under its crust of filth, with its crumpled eyelids, the face had lost all semblance of humanity; how could they waken thought behind that hideous mask? Perken grasped the man's shoulders.

"What . . . what's happened?"

The man did not turn towards Perken, near though he was, but to the light. His cheeks twitched; he was about to speak again. Shuddering at what he expected to hear, Claude waited for the answer. At last—a single word!

"Nothing. . . ."

The man was not insane; he had lingered on the word as if he groped for other words to add. Obviously it was not that memory failed him, or that he would not answer; this was . . . *his truth!* And yet —the words had stamped themselves on Claude's imagination—this man had said: "Things can't go any further than the muzzle of my revolver; I got my way out ready!" But now, to all intents, the man was dead. Something had to be resuscitated in this corpse, as artificial respiration brings back life to a drowned body.

The door swung to. Darkness closed in on them again, cleft by a single shaft of light, like a ray falling from the loophole of a dungeon. Claude's mind was all an agonizing question: "Were the Mois, *those same Mois,* surrounding them?" Then suddenly he realized the darkness that encompassed them, the airless darkness of a prison cell. Hurling himself at the door, he flung it wide open and looked back. Startled by the rush of light, the man staggered a

159

pace forward with the nervous jerk of a terrified animal. The bell tinkled. The sudden light, the sound of voices, had called a reflex into play. Perken went to the door and picked up a wooden stave which had fallen in the rectangle of sunlight just after Claude flung the door open. It was a sort of goad, a stick tipped with a bamboo spike of the same kind as the war-spikes. Turning, he expected to see Grabot's back, but Grabot had swung round towards him. Taking his knife from his pocket, he began to cut the thongs, as far away as possible from the man's arms. The knots were primitive but efficient, and it was no easy matter cutting through them. To cut the trace he had to come close up to Grabot. At last the man was free, but he did not move.

"You can move now, old chap."

Grabot started moving along his old track, parallel with the wall, lunging clumsily forward. Suddenly he stumbled and all but fell. Hardly conscious of his gesture, Perken swung him round a little to the left and began pushing him towards the door. Grabot stopped again; he had only just realized that his shoulders were free. Then he felt before him with his hand—his first gesture showing unmistakably that he was blind. Now that he had finished with the thongs, Perken let his hand drop on to the cross-bar; it touched the bell. Slashing through the fastening, he flung it angrily towards the door. As the bell dropped, jangling, on the ground, the blind man's mouth fell open—with amazement, it seemed. Perken's eyes had followed the direction of the sound and he observed some Mois a few yards away trying to peer into the hut. Some were crouching, and there were several rows of heads; they had evidently turned out in force.

"The first thing to do," Claude said, "is to get out of this place."

"Keep your eyes shut while you're going out, or you'll be dazzled, and if you show the least hesitation, they'll be on you like a knife!"

But at this moment nothing in the world could have made Claude shut his eyes; he felt that, if he did so, he might never open them again. He launched himself into the sunlight, his eyes fixed on the ground, straining every nerve to prevent himself from stopping. The line of Mois gave way, retreated. Only one remained; convinced this man must be the master of the slave, Perken went up to him.

"Phya," he said. Shrugging his shoulders, the Moi went away.

"What's that you said?"

"*'Phya'*—it means 'chief.' It's the word our interpreter was always using. Just as well to play up to him—it may be useful later on. But what's become of Grabot, damn it?"

The blind man was standing on the threshold of the hut. In the full light of day he looked more horrible than ever. Perken went up to him and took him by the arm.

"Come along to our hut," he said.

The Mois followed them.

3

They looked into the chief's hut; nobody was there. Still hanging on the wall, in semi-darkness, was the white drill jacket. A little way off the Mois had gathered round them in a half circle. Perken singled out the one who had acted as their guide.

"Where is the chief?"

The Moi hesitated, as if hostilities had already begun. At last he decided to speak.

"Gone. Back this evening."

"Is it a lie?" Claude asked Perken.

"Better get back to our hut, before anything else." They each took one of Grabot's arms. "No," Perken continued, "I hardly think it's a lie. My questions about a white chief flustered him, most likely. In the circumstances he's probably gone off as a precaution

—to make sure that in case of need he can count on the help of neighboring villages."

"In a word, we've walked into a trap?"

"Well, things have taken a nasty turn. . . . Still it's not our doing."

They were speaking across Grabot's corpse-like profile.

"Wouldn't it be best to push off before he gets back?" Claude asked.

"Dangerous as these Mois are, the jungle's even worse."

Still, Claude reflected, even so, shouldn't they set off at once, abandoning their stores, the stones . . . ? But they'd need a guide, otherwise their chances of surviving were—*nil.*

Xa greeted them at the hut with a look confessing terror, but little surprise.

"Well, shall we yoke the bullocks?" Claude asked.

Perken measured with his eyes the height of the wooden ramparts, and shrugged his shoulders.

"They're mobilizing . . ." he said.

The group of Mois had not continued following them. Others, who were armed, had joined the group. And once again, as if nothing could subdue the onset of the forest and its forms of life, Claude felt himself transported into an insect-world. From the scattered huts which, only a moment before, were silent and seemingly unoccupied, now, through invisible exits, a swarm of Mois was emerging; with nimble, wasp-like movements they streamed along the path, brandishing their mantis-like weapons. Now and again the spears and cross-bows stood out against the sky clean-cut as waving antennæ. And still more men poured from the huts. They did not speak; the only sound that came from their direction was the padding of bare feet on the low brushwood. The squeal of a black pig echoed across the village, and died down again. Once more the silence merged into the sunlight; only the stealthy footfalls of the savages beat on the windless air.

The two white men and Xa had entered the hut, taking with them their weapons and all the ammunition. The carts, from one of which a stone protruded, were still in sight. Could the hut, which stood on stilt-like piles, be fortified in any way? A wattle lay on the floor. They stood it up on end and realized at once that, as it was only a yard high, it would not serve for cover much above the thighs. If arrows came over they would have to lie flat. And the hut was flimsy as the temporary booths erected at a country fair. Looking across the open space in front of them—a sort of village square—they could see, through gaps between the huts and shade-trees, the Mois moving to and fro within a second vast rectangle of open ground, lying along the palisade. Completely deserted now, the open zone immediately before them seemed to interpose a frail bulwark between them and the silent menace of the Mois.

"Look here, Grabot," Perken said, "you know these people, don't you? We're in the hut to the right of the chief's. They seem to be preparing to make a move—what's their game, do you think? . . . Damn it, you might answer! You understand me, don't you?"

Silence. A mosquito droned in Perken's ear, and, in sheer exasperation, he slapped his own cheek viciously. At last a voice came, Grabot's.

"What the hell can it matter?"

"Want to stay here for ever, do you?"

Grabot shook his head, but the movement looked meaningless. Without the expression of an eye to reinforce it, the jerk of his neck seemed merely brutish—like a bull's; brutish, too, his hardly human voice.

"What the hell can it matter . . . now?"

"Now that you . . . that you're . . ."

"That . . . everything, damn it!"

"Perhaps something can be done. . . ."

"And what about the blasted dogs they got to wolf my eye? Something can be done about *them*, eh?"

A line of tapered points had risen into view in the offing; on the far side of the open space more spearmen had assembled.

"Who's in the hut? There's you. That other fellow's some youngster, I guess. Who's the third one?"

"The boy."

"That all? And they—are they surrounding us?"

"Wait a bit! I can only see in front."

With two quick jabs of his knife he punctured

small holes in each of the side-walls and peered through them.

"No, there aren't any at the sides."

"There will be. When it's dark, all they've got to do is to light a fire underneath. That's the way they did me in. But what the hell can it matter?"

There was another silence. The frieze of spears had sunk out of sight. The tribesmen were evidently squatting on the ground, waiting.

"How's one to get anything out of him?" Claude asked himself.

Perken turned to Grabot again.

"Do you want to be butchered here?" he asked.

He shook his fists—fists that Grabot could not see. He was as much a prisoner now in his private universe of forms as Grabot in the darkness of his eyeless head. How did one argue with a blind man? He closed his own eyes, pressing the lids together, groping for words to say. Grabot began speaking.

"If you get hold of one of them, just turn him over to me. Trussed up. . . ."

Claude had been watching a spear that had just risen into view, but Grabot's voice startled him so profoundly that he forgot about the spear. There was such sheer ferocity in his words, they rose from some unfathomable depth of humiliation. He did not find them bestial so much as horrible—yet, at the same time, simplicity itself. Was this human spirit, which in the hut nothing so far had roused from apathy, reviving now only to grow aware of

166

its appalling degradation? Claude could guess the dreams of torture haunting the twilight of the blind man's mind; his fingers were gathered to a point, the nails clustering together, groping for an eye to grind out of existence. His arm was steady; only his hand shook. His face betrayed no feeling, but his toes were twitching. Not his lips, but the man's body spoke. Claude remembered how, the moment they had entered the hut containing the grindstone, that hand had begged for food, that back had winced from an impending goad. But it was a body that spoke only of its sufferings. So compelling was its wordless language that for a second Claude forgot that it was they whom tortures now awaited yonder. For, should the Mois decide to burn them out, they would be helpless. Helpless. . . . A peacock's cry shrilled through the silence, died out upon the tranquil air. The squatting Mois might have been dozing, but for their hawk-like, watchful eyes, and, above them, the very air seemed tense and charged with menace, like a hawk hovering, motionless, above his quarry. As long as daylight lasted. . . .

"D'you think they'll set the place on fire, Perken?"

"Sure of it."

Grabot had relapsed into silence.

"They're waiting, either for the chief's return, or for the darkness. Or for both. Yes, old chap, they've got us, and they know it."

(For a moment Claude thought the "old chap" was for Grabot.)

167

"In that case," Claude said, "wouldn't it be better to blaze away at them and make a dash for the gate? We've plenty of cartridges. It's a hundred to one chance, of course. But very likely we could put the wind up them enough to . . ."

"To begin with, by the time we'd brought down a couple of them, the rest would all have scurried under cover. And then, once you start that game, any more parleying's out of the question. You never know—they may consider we've violated the rice-spirit oath by rescuing Grabot, but they're not quite sure about it, I imagine. And, don't forget, they'd be even more dangerous out there in the forest than they are here."

"If we're goners anyhow, I'd like to do in a few of the swine first. Look there's two of them outside this hole and four, five—no, six, eight—more, most likely, on the other side. Cheerful outlook, eh? Suppose we tried a dash in that direction? After all there's only the stockade to cross."

"There's the forest, too."

Claude made no reply. Perken became aware of a curious noise outside: a low rumble as if a boiler were being rolled along the ground.

"They won't try lighting a fire before it's dark," he remarked after awhile. "Our only hope is to make a dash for it then. The thing is to fight them under cover of darkness, before they. . . ."

"By God, wouldn't I like to let the daylight into some of those brutes! That fellow over there strolling along by himself, for instance—I can feel my revolver pricking up its ears! Sure we oughtn't to present him with one of these?" He tapped the cartridges in the magazine. "There'll always be two left."

"Wha-at?" a harsh voice drawled.

Grabot had spoken at last. Only one voice could have put such concentrated venom into a single word —the voice of the blind man beside them. There was more than bitterness in it; a deep conviction, too. Startled, Claude turned and looked at the man again. His skin was an unhealthy gray, the complexion of a dweller underground, but he had a wrestler's shoulders. A wreck, but a mighty wreck. And he had once been more than brave. But, as on the temples, Asia had set her mark on him; he, too, had fallen on evil days. Yet this man had had the temerity to destroy one of his eyes, and to explore these perilous regions without the least safe-conduct. "At the worst things can't go further than the muzzle of my revolver." No less than the Mois Grabot inspired him now with infinite horror.

"But, blast it all, surely a man can . . . !"

"Damn fool!"

More eloquently than the insult, and even than his voice, the jerk of Grabot's mutilated head conveyed his meaning. "You can't when it's unnecessary, and when it's necessary—it may be too late to act." Surely, Claude thought, a man has only to make up his mind. But, for Grabot, evidently, Claude's opinion on such an issue hardly counted. Hooking his

169

wrist, Claude raised his revolver and pointed the muzzle at his own head. As he did so, he realized how absurd the gesture was; he knew that, if it came to firing, in that last moment he would aim not at himself but Grabot—if only for the satisfaction of wiping out that face of hate incarnate, and annihilating that reminder of his own human lot, as a murderer lops off his tell-tale finger. Then, suddenly aware of the weight of the revolver on his wrist, he let his arm drop. The feeling of absurdity surged back from him like a spent wave and, as it fell away, the hostile shadows massed in the background, the spears and the great horns outlined against the sky, seemed for the first time unimportant. But only for a second. For then one of the Mois stood up and, stumbling, clutched at his neighbor, who gave a sudden cry. Muted by the distance, the sound traveled slowly over the open space, ousting its aspect of a latent ambush. In the offing the Mois were steadily growing more numerous. But, whether they squatted down or moved about, whether they carried bows or spears, none of them ventured beyond the limit of the empty foreground. They huddled in a serried, seething mass, like a pack of hounds or wolves, penned behind an invisible line, as if some occult power forbade their crossing it. In the emptiness before the white men nothing stirred; time alone lived in it, meting out their fate. The passing minutes seemed immured within the ring-fence of those bestial faces, in which eternity was incarnate—an obdurate barrier that nothing happening in the outside world could cross, nothing could permeate. It seemed to Claude as if to live, and to watch the progress of the prisoned hours—worst of all the coming of that hour in which the sky would pale and twilight usher in their holocaust—could only mean ever to grow more cruelly aware that they were hemmed in by a barrier of living beings aligned before another barrier, the towering stockade; each hour was bringing them a clearer and still clearer realization that their detention was but the prelude to slavery. They were like animals at bay. A horde of beasts of prey, the Mois watched them, biding their time to spring; only their eyes seemed alive, fixed on the hut as on a baited trap. Whenever Claude focused his glasses on a head, he caught at once the man's eyes peering at him. When he put the glasses down, though he could no longer see their glint, their look of feral hunger, the vision lingered—of staring eyes slotted between puckered lids, of craning, dog-like necks.

Some more warriors had come into view—they looked like duplicates of the first group—and were leaning on their cross-bows. These late arrivals crept forward in a file like ants, and they, too, kept behind the cabalistic line, but further to the left. One side of the hut partly concealed them. Perken punctured another hole in the wall and discovered, almost touching it, a grave surmounted by two large fetishes with projecting teeth; they represented a man and a woman, each clutching its red-dyed sexual organs with both hands. Beyond the grave there was another hut. Evidently the Mois were advancing behind this hut and meant to occupy it. Nothing, however, could be seen of their movements, as wattles had been placed across the openings. The Mois vanished behind the hut as if a trap-door were swallowing them up; wave after wave advanced and disappeared from view. They were pouring into the hut from the other side, and, behind the closely barricaded wall, beyond the wooden sexual organs and the clutching fingers, the whole hut was buzzing like a wasps' nest. For all its air of close-sealed immobility the façade gave the impression of being alive, and darkly hostile. It was instinct with the secret life of all the sub-human creatures vanishing behind it, their unseen menace.

"What's their idea?" Claude whispered. "Is it simply to get nearer us?"

"There wouldn't be so many of them. . . . Wait!"

Perken picked up the binoculars. Almost immediately he motioned with his hand, beckoning to Claude,—then brought it back at once, to steady the glasses. After a while he passed them to Claude.

"Look at the corners."

"Well?"

"Lower down, near the floor."

"What do you mean? The things sticking out, or those holes they've made?"

"It's the same idea. The things sticking out are cross-bows. The holes are loopholes to take more bows."

"Well?"

"I've counted over twenty of them."

"But, if we start firing, the wattles won't be much protection for those chaps!"

"They'll be lying flat. Most of our bullets will go wide. What's more, it will be dark and they'll be able to see us because our hut will be on fire. But we'll hardly be able to see anything."

"But why have they taken all that trouble? They'd have been just as well off where they were."

"Their idea is to get us *alive*."

Again Claude stared at the huge war-machine; he could not take his eyes off the curved bows projecting like a row of wooden beaks along the lower margin of the wall. Xa was talking to Perken, but he hardly heard his voice. Perken took the field-glasses and leveled them in the other direction, towards the far end of the open space. Then he handed them to Claude, who examined the same spot. Many of the Mois, he noticed, were bending down, and moved as if they were bedding out young plants; the others walked warily, flexing their knees and lifting each foot in turn high in the air, like cats. He cast an enquiring glance at Perken.

"They're planting war-spikes," Perken said.

Obviously they were waiting for the nightfall, and taking their precautions accordingly. And, he did not doubt, similar operations were in progress behind the hut, behind the ant-like lines of crouching men.

There could be no question of preventing the

Mois from setting fire to the hut. Once the fire had caught, they could only dash out straight ahead and face the cross-bows, or else swerve to the right, where the war-spikes awaited them. And, even if they got through, there would still be the stockade to cross and, after it, the forest. . . . No, there was nothing they could do—except kill as many Mois as possible. He remembered the way the leeches squirmed and shriveled up when he burnt them alive on the end of a match.

They could do nothing except what Perken had suggested, and try to make a dash for it under cover of the dusk, just before the hut was set on fire. And then they would have the jungle to face. But what chance had they of getting through as far as that with all the war-spikes on the way . . . ?

Claude glanced towards the carts. The carts . . . the stones. Yes, they'd have to begin all over again. But the first thing was to get out of here alive; failing that, to get oneself killed. At all costs, not to be taken alive.

"What are they sticking in the ground now?"

In the distance the tribesmen were giving signs of renewed activity. Their spears were crossed.

"No, they're not planting anything. That means the chief is back."

Perken passed the glasses to Claude. Now that he saw them more distinctly, he recognized that the Mois' movements were ordered. Nothing could distract the savages from their set purpose. All the malignant tension of the air, the brooding hostility of men and things, seemed converging from the watching crowd on the four men at bay within the hut. It beat upon them like the impact of a single hostile will. And, suddenly, that spirit of malignity seemed to have found its counterpart—in Perken. He stood there like an automaton, his mouth was gaping, all expression had left his face, his eyes were fixed in a vacant stare. Nothing human remained in the hut. Xa was lying in a corner, curled up like an animal. Grabot—well, Grabot had better keep his mouth shut! Outside—a sea of bestial faces, creatures of savage cruelty, as little human, as implacable as the gaur's skull with its grinning death's-head teeth. And now, inside, was Perken—a man of stone. The panic fear that comes of utter, overwhelming loneliness gripped Claude in the pit of the stomach, in the hollow of his back. The panic of a man left to his fate amongst a crowd of madmen about to leap on him. He dared not speak, but placed his hand on Perken's shoulder. Perken brushed it away without looking at him, took two steps forward and halted full in the opening, within easy arrow-shot.

"Take care!"

But Perken was beyond listening. . . . So here the long adventure of his life was to find quietus, here in a pool of steaming blood, or in that last infirmity of courage which had brought Grabot low. Here, too, it seemed, there was no escaping from the forest's dark dominion. Claude glanced at Grabot. His head sunk

175

on his chest, his long hair straggling about his face, the blind man was shambling round and round the hut as if he still were harnessed to the mill-stone. One shoulder was thrust forward. He had gone back to servitude again.

Perken, too, was haunted by a face—his own to-morrow. He saw the lids drawn tight over his eyes . . . for ever. But—a man could always put up a fight. And—kill! That jungle yonder was not merely a ferment of virulent malignity; it had trees and thickets from behind which a man could shoot. Or starve to death. The pangs of hunger—he had experience of them, he knew their frenzied agony; but that was nothing, nothing beside the death-in-life of the slave strapped to the slowly turning grindstone day after day after day. And then, in the jungle, a man can kill himself, without fuss or flurry. . . .

But the insistent menace of all those watchful faces made lucid thought impossible. One last, clear vision loomed in his mind: the infinite humiliation of a man caught in the snare of his appointed fate. Grappling with the prescience of his degradation, he felt a rush of sensual rage sweep over him, like an orgasm, intensified by the sight of Grabot tramping mechanically round the hut, circling the corpse of his own courage. A grotesque notion flashed across his mind—of the punishments assigned to Pride—a vision of himself with mangled, twisted limbs, head lolling backwards like a shouldered pack, and his body like a stake driven into the earth. He felt an insensate longing that such torments should exist, so that, in their extremity, a man might be enabled to spit in the face of torture, and defy it with full consciousness, with all his will, though it should make him shriek with agony. And such was his wild elation at the thought that he was risking more than death, so vividly did he see it as his revenge upon the universe, his warrant of release from man's estate, that he was conscious of an inward struggle, an effort to fight down an overpowering hallucination, a kind of ecstasy. No man . . . can hold out . . against torture. The sentence jangled in his brain, somehow associated with a curious rattling noise. His teeth were chattering. He climbed the wattle, hesitated one second more, fell, pulled himself up, and stood still, one arm held up above his head, grasping his revolver butt-foremost, as if it were a peace-offering.

Mad . . . ? Claude held his breath, covering Perken with his own weapon. Perken had begun to walk deliberately in the direction of the Mois, his whole body rigid. The sunset cast long, level shadows on the clearing, kindling a last faint light on the revolver-butt. Perken could no longer see his way; his foot caught in a low shrub. He made a movement with his hand as if to brush it aside—he was off the footpath—and then went on, sank on to one knee, and got up, rigid as ever, holding up the revolver as before. So viciously did the thorns prick him that for a second he saw what lay in front of him. The chief was insistently pointing to the ground. He was to drop the revolver. Looking up, he saw it above his head. With an effort he crooked his arm and grasped the revolver in his other hand as if he intended to wrench it away. There was no longer any question of hesitation; he simply could not move. At last his hand dropped suddenly, and opened, every finger spread. The revolver fell.

He took a few more steps. Never before had he walked like this, without flexing the knee. The power that controlled his movements knew little of his bones. Were he not conscious of the driving force that urged him like a fascinated animal towards his torturers, he would have fancied he was moving aimlessly. Each movement of his rigid legs reverberated in his loins and neck. Every tuft of grass scraped from the ground by his feet—he could not see them— seemed clamping him to the soil, intensifying the resistance of his body; his weight fell heavily on either leg in turn with a jarring impact that hampered the next step. As he approached, the Mois lowered their spears and pointed them towards him; the spearheads glimmered faintly in the dying light. It struck him suddenly that the Mois not only blinded their slaves but castrated them as well.

Once again he realized that he was riveted to the spot, mastered by his flesh, his sinews—by all that can rebel against man. It was not fear that paralysed him, for he knew he would persist in his dogged advance. Fate, it seemed, could do more and worse than break his courage down. Most likely, he reflected, Grabot was twice a corpse. (What about his beard, though?) He had a grotesque impulse to turn and take another look at the fellow. When he turned he only saw the revolver. It was lying near the path, almost in the middle of a patch of clay so bare it seemed as if the weapon had burnt up the grass around it. Well, it could account for seven of those men; could hold its own in a tight corner. It looked alive. He began walking back to it. There was a flash in the red dusk . . . the gleaming wooden crescents of the cross-bows.

It flashed on him that there was a world of vaster horror, a world of worse things than those gouged-out eyes, worse even than castration. . . . Madness was like the forest which from its brief frontier here stretched out interminably. Still he was not mad, as yet. A tragic exaltation, savage ecstasy, swept over him. He was still looking towards his feet. And, staring at his tattered gaiters and twisted laces, he seemed to see, fantastically imaged on their surface, an old picture, the likeness of a barbarian prince, a prisoner like himself, who, cast alive into a barrel of vipers, died roaring out his war-song, his furious fists beating the air like bursting knots. His skin was tingling with mingled fear and resolution. He gave the revolver a kick; it hopped along for a yard or two like a toad. Then he began to move again towards the Mois.

Like a rifleman following a moving target along

his sights, Claude kept him in the circle of his glasses, panting with excitement. Would the Mois shoot? He tried to see their faces, but they were a little out of focus and, without pausing to adjust the glasses, he brought them back to Perken, who was walking on exactly as before, his chest well forward, his back arched like a coolie's hauling a boat, his arms invisible, his legs as stiff as ramrods. When he turned round Claude had seen his face again, but only long enough to notice that his mouth was open. He guessed from the rigidity of his body and the way his shoulders jerked forward at every step, as if they were actuated by a machine, that his eyes, too, must be set in a fixed, automatic stare. For a moment Perken occupied the whole field of his binoculars. Then the field began to drift away towards the left; with a quick movement of his wrist he centered it again. Once more he lost sight of Perken and found that he was looking for him too far ahead, in a long streak of sunset light. Perken had just stopped.

For a moment the line of Mois on which Perken was advancing seemed devoid of depth. Only their heads showed up, the lower portions of their bodies melted into a gray mist slowly rising from the ground. Above them hovered a last, uncertain ray of light; its tremulous vibrations seemed allied with the quivering suspense of the dark bodies against the vast serenity of the dusk. Perken's empty hand, limp and light as a sick man's, was clenched as if it closed about a phantom weapon. Suddenly he raised his eyes towards the tree-tops lit by the dying splendor of the sunset, and the contrast between that beauty and the dark, seething immobility of the savage crowd below fretted his heart with longing for the liberty that was escaping him. Poised on the brink of that loathsome transformation, his mind obsessed with it, he clung to his natural self; his clenched fists bruised the soft flesh of his thighs, his eyes seemed far too small to take in all the visible world, his skin grew taut to breaking-point. To his dying freedom he clung with the wild passion of a lover clasping his dying mistress, and in the shadow of its dissolution his will blazed up in a last orgasm of supreme intensity; he moved along the avenue of death, his eyes held by the level ray of sunlight lengthening, lengthening out above the trees. It drew his spirit out of reach of all the evil presences below, the phantoms lurking in the earth-bound darkness. Then, suddenly, the red glow paled, grew wraith-like, scattering up the sky, and the brief dusk that heralds in the sudden nightfall of the tropics fell in a dust of darkness on the clearing. The bodies of the Mois coalesced; only the frieze of spears emerged, black on a sky grown colorless and dead. Perken fell back into the world of men. Once more he was confronting their ferocity, facing the malignant menace of the spears. . . . Then something happened; the universe seemed tottering above his head, he heard his own voice rising in a cry, felt something clutching at his heart. Death? No . . . ; he felt the panic ebbing from his mind but in his body pain persisted. He was wounded. The smell of grass was in his nostrils. Then he understood. He had fallen, one foot impaled on a war-spike, and, in falling, had been lacerated on other spikes. Blood was oozing from his wrist. He picked himself up, propping himself on his hands. Then he realized that he was wounded in the knee. The Mois had hardly moved, yet somehow they seemed nearer. Had they begun to charge and been held back? In the gloom all he could plainly see was the whites of their eyes, for all their restlessness intently fixed on him. Very near him now. A pack. Did one of them leap forward, he would be within spear-thrust. Pain, acute yet numbing pain, welled up in him. Yet, somehow, he felt liberated from himself; he was returning to the surface. The Mois were grasping their spears in both hands, holding them across their chests—as they hold them when they engage with a wild beast. And he was panting like an animal at bay. His small revolver was still in his pocket. Should he shoot the chief without drawing? And after that— what next? He could not rest his weight on the wounded leg; steadying himself on the other, he let it dangle, but the weight of his foot dragged it down, and a sharp, scalding twinge shot through his knee. The pain rose in a steady rhythm, in sickening waves of agony; somehow it was connected with his pulse, drumming in his head, across his temples. Pain had quickened his perceptions and now he was conscious that the Mois had made another move. A group had passed behind him, cutting him off from Claude. That might explain their willingness to let him come so near. . . .

4

Perken halted, facing the Mois. The chief kept his eyes fixed on him, watching for his next move; the restless flicker of his eyelids gave a curious vacillation to his gaze. Perken's uninjured hand, the right, still clasped the little revolver in his pocket, ready to press the trigger at the first sign of an attack; he was handicapped by a persistent impulse to drag the pocket upwards, as if by doing so he could have eased the pressure on his wounded leg. He stretched out his left hand towards the guide, who was standing beside the chief. As his arm went up the Moi swung his saber round towards the outstretched hand—he had not realized that Perken's gesture was pacific. The saber all but touched the fingers, whence blood was trickling soundlessly, drop by drop, on to the ground, before it was let fall.

"Do you know that man is worth a hundred jars?" Perken shouted.

The guide did not interpret, and a sense of impotence swept over Perken suddenly, appallingly. His fingers itched to grip the savage by the neck, to shake the words out of that gaping mouth!

"Interpret, damn you!"

The guide stared blankly at him, with a cringing movement of his head; the words seemed to intimidate him more than would have done a violent gesture. It dawned on Perken that the man had failed to understand him; he had spoken too quickly and in a pure Siamese to which the guide was unaccustomed. By raising his voice, moreover, he had blurred the difference between the tones. He made another attempt, speaking now with careful deliberateness.

"You—tell—chief. . . ."

He spaced out the words, irritated by his rapid breathing that jerked each syllable out of his mouth. His eyes were fixed on the interpreter's, trying to read his thoughts. The man's bestial, impassive gaze disconcerted him. The Moi inclined his shoulder slightly towards the chief, as if he were preparing to speak.

"Blind—white—man—worth. . . ."

Did he understand? Perken wondered. His fate, his future, were staked on that lump of squalid flesh. All the years of his life had served but to bring him to

this pass, to confront him with that sub-human creature, versed like the wild beasts of the jungle only in
ruse and treachery, that body scabbed with eczema
and girdled with a filthy, blood-stained loin-cloth!
On this creature and on its rudimentary mind he
depended utterly; on the embryonic thoughts which
in the dark recesses of its skull were squirming into
life, like flies' eggs hatching in a dead man's brain.
More than ever during the past hour, he felt a passionate desire to kill. . . . He steadied his voice.

"Worth—more—than—hundred—jars."

At last! The man was beginning to translate. The
old chief made no gesture. Such was the stillness of
the savages that everywhere all movement seemed
suspended, but for the darkness visibly creeping up
the sky. As it had been during the ceremony of the
forenoon, so now it seemed that all the life of this
far, isolated corner of the earth hung on the silent
shadow of the chief. No sound of life came from the
vast spaces of the forest which, like a waveless tide,
flooded the world up to the furthest limit with its
unfathomable silence. Perken still looked for a gesture; none was forthcoming. The chief moved nearer
to the interpreter and spoke to him. The man translated at once.

"More than a hundred?"

"More."

The chief pondered; his teeth were moving, nib-
bling like a rabbit's. Suddenly he looked up, startled
by a sudden cry.

"Perken!"

Claude had lost sight of Perken and was calling to him. In a few minutes it would be quite dark, and with the passing of the light their last hope of escape would have vanished.

"Come here!" Perken shouted with all his might.

Again there was a silence. The chief was eyeing him mistrustfully, resentfully, his gums still teetering. Perken addressed the interpreter again.

"Say I'm telling him to come."

"Unarmed," the chief commanded.

Perken shouted to Claude in French. "Bring only your little browning."

The issue still was hanging in the balance.

As Perken's voice died out upon the grayish shadows enveloping the hut, a disk of light peered through them; Claude had switched on his electric torch. Nothing could be seen of him, and his feet moved soundlessly across the undergrowth; the only evidence of his approach was the disk of light advancing, always at the same height from the ground, in rapid zigzags. Its movement to and fro seemed timed to the fluent throb of blood in Perken's temples, which, try as he might, he could not quell. The light was following the footpath, it seemed. Suddenly it shot up from the ground and swept across the faces of the savages; then, as it sank to earth again, feeling for the track, all the dim figures bending towards Perken, the white flash of their teeth, which for a

186

moment had held his eyes, fell back into the darkness.

Perken's wounds were growing painful; with an effort he seated himself on the ground, and the twinges became less frequent. The electric torch went out. Now Claude was only a few yards off; his footfalls could be heard upon the leaves. His legs stretched out, his head close to the ground, Perken could only see the dark mass of the forest into which all nearer forms were merged, and the row of spears outlined against the sky. A sound of muted voices drifted towards him; a furtive confabulation was in progress. Then he heard Claude speaking.

"Are you wounded?"

"No. Well, yes—but it's nothing serious. Sit down beside me. Don't light your torch."

The Mois were piling faggots for a fire. Perken explained what he had said to them.

"So you offered them over a hundred jars," Claude said. "How many warriors are there, do you think?"

"Somewhere between one and two hundred."

"They seem to be wrangling amongst themselves. Any idea what it's about?"

The voices had grown more guttural and two of them dominated all the others; harsh, peremptory voices. One was the chief's.

"The chief and Grabot's owner are having it out between them, I imagine."

"Who's on the chief's side? The whole village, d'you think?"

"I expect so."

"Supposing," Claude suggested, "we offer a jar to each warrior and five or ten—you decide how many —to the village?"

Perken made the proposal at once. No sooner had the interpreter translated it than a buzz of voices filled the darkness. All the Mois had begun talking at once, at first in undertones, then in a shrill, excited gabble. The spears flickered to and fro across a sky bright with the selfsame stars that they had watched the previous night. Suddenly the spears became invisible; flames had begun to leap up from the pile of faggots, hissing and spluttering, and rose-pink waves of tremulous light were breaking on the darkness. As the flames rose higher the tribesmen's heads loomed out, the front row clearly visible, the others hidden in shadows. Almost all the warriors were gathered there, gabbling like madmen, all but forgetful of the white men's presence. Each spoke for himself, spoke loud and still more loudly, gesticulating only with his head, his arms at rest. At regular intervals the fire broke into a blaze; sweeping across the din of voices thrumming like muffled castanets, the firelight spread a glowing patina upon the Mois' faces. But for the eyes where, quicker even than the leaping flame, a glint of furtive, hawk-like wariness flashed into intermittent view, they might have been the faces of old peasants. Within the noisy group there was a zone of silence, where the elders were squatting round the chief, dangling their long, ape-like arms.

Each of them spoke in turn. Claude kept his eyes on them, trying his utmost to interpret the expression of their faces; but they were inscrutable, as foreign to him as the tongue in which they spoke.

The interpreter walked up to Perken and addressed him.

"One of you will go, the other stay till he returns."

"No."

Claude had the interpreter explain that if one of them went alone he well might perish on the way—in which case the barter could not take place.

The Mois conferred again. Claude turned to Perken.

"In the last resort . . ." he began.

"No, I know their mentality. If we've whetted their appetites, the elders won't be able to stand out against the village. The great thing is to gain time. If only it were daylight, I'd find some way of tackling them."

Suddenly the loud chattering died down into a gentle murmur, like the twittering of a flight of birds as they take wing. All eyes were turned towards the group of elders, and mouths which, in the intervals of conversation, had stayed agape, now closed discreetly.

"No tribe possesses one jar for each man," Perken shouted in Siamese.

The interpreter translated. The chief kept silence, no one moved; heavy with foreboding, suspense seemed spreading on the air, like water-rings upon a lake. All the warriors were staring at the chief. Perken had half a mind to stand up, but feared he might walk unsteadily and weaken thus the impact of his words. He shouted again.

"We will come without an escort. The jars . . ." The interpreter moved towards him and with one accord all the dark heads veered round, to follow his advance. ". . . the jars will be brought in carts. No escort. Understand?"

He paused after each sentence, so as to have it translated at once.

"Only three of us. Have the exchange made in any clearing you choose."

Claude was so used to seeing white men nod assent that the utter immobility of all the faces confronting him—coming so soon after their swerve in the direction of the guide—struck him as a refusal. "Still that should appeal to them," he whispered, "the idea of having a jar each."

"It hasn't soaked in yet."

There was a slight stir amongst the Mois. Some had risen and were standing as if uncertain what to do, their backs still bent, an arm—the arm on which each had been leaning—dangling towards the ground. Then, preceded by their shadows, three or four of them began to move off towards the hut whence the white men had come. They merged into the darkness of the trees; only the tips of their spears showed up against the skyline. The other Mois waited, and so contagious was their suspense that the white men felt it gaining on them, too. Claude kept his eyes fixed on the sinuous horizon of the tree-tops, waiting to see above it the returning spears. The emissaries raised a shout; their news was greeted with a chorus of approval. The spearheads showed up for a moment, crossed, beside a glowing star, sank out of sight, shot up again, grown larger in proximity. At last the men stepped into the zone of firelight, linked to the outer darkness by their shadows trailing away behind them. Perken recognized Grabot's master amongst them; evidently he had gone to the hut to make sure that his slave was still there; the Mois had feared he might have run away. He was trying to go back to the hut, but his two companions held him by the wrists. All three were talking excitedly, but Perken had no idea what they were saying. At last they squatted down and the palavering began again; there was a strangely pastoral air about it all—like the confabulations of a group of rustics— that veiled to some extent its underlying savagery.

"Will it last long?" Claude asked.

"Till they put out the fire, at dawn. That's their custom; dawn's the lucky moment for making a decision."

Now that the strain on his energy was relaxed, Perken was thrown back upon himself. He was hardly conscious that his life had been given back to him; when he had challenged torture and utter degradation, fearing he could not stand against them, he had been so violently lifted out of himself that now he

191

seemed to face merely a world of shadows, the figments of a dream. What reality could there be in that drone of voices rising and falling with the leaping flames, in this colloquy of madmen in the heart of darkness, amid the overwhelming silence of the forest? As his fever rose, an immense hatred surged up in him, hatred of mankind, of life, of all the forces that were mastering him again and scattering the wild memories of that terrific moment, like the lost splendor of a vision. He had ceased to realize he was a prisoner; more insistent than conscious thought, his fever and the throbbing of his wound pervaded all his being, and the heat-mist hovering on his cheeks and temples was disintegrating his perception of the world of men.

The Mois had ceased moving. Each burst of firelight lit up the selfsame lances planted in the soil, casting a sudden sheen on the same sweating arms. Like a buzzing swarm of insects circling over squatting mummies, a thin drone of voices floated above the crowd of savages, hidden for the most part in obscurity. When the flames died down the shadows broke in heavy waves upon them; only the spears stood out, like spars out of a tangled mass of jetsam. Perken's fever was rising still and to his burning eyes the Mois seemed like rigid forms of stone, barbaric effigies on which the darkness sprawled, engulfing them as the forest swallowed up the ruined temples; then from the ebbing tide of darkness once more the ranks of stony heads emerged, pitted with vitreous eyes red-glowing in the firelight up to the furthest limit of its range.

At the first ray of dawn a clod of earth crushed out the last flame of the fire. The interpreter came up and squatted beside Perken.

"You will fix the date and the place."

"On oath?"

"On oath."

The interpreter transmitted the brief dialogue at the top of his voice. One by one, the Mois rose; in the cold gray light they looked like the draggled survivors of a shipwreck. The clotted mass of them heaved like an awning in a breeze; then gradually fell asunder. Some of them made water where they stood.

"Sure we can trust the oath, Perken?"

"Wait a bit! Would you go and fetch the cartridges in my old holster—it's in the first cart, under my jacket—and my Colt?"

"Where is it?"

"Can't say exactly. Somewhere between this and the hut."

Fortunately the revolver had fallen on a bare patch of earth; Claude discovered it at once. As he picked it up a fully dressed native came out of the hut. It was Xa. Somehow his coming seemed a reassurance. They went to the carts together; Xa found the holster and brought it to Perken.

"Where's Grabot?" Perken asked.

193

"Him sleeping now," the boy replied.

The elders were squatting under the gaur's head. A slave brought up the jars of rice-spirit. Perken rose, steadying himself on Claude's shoulder. The sight of his unshaven cheeks, sunken and quivering, startled Claude; Perken was biting his lips so as not to betray his agony on his face. The chief drank from the jar and proffered the bamboo. As Perken was bringing his lips down to it, he seemed to hesitate. All eyes were fixed on him.

"What's up?" Claude asked.

"Wait . . . !"

Had he refused to take the oath? The Mois eyed the chief, waiting for a signal. Perken had raised his hand, inviting their attention. "Watch the gaur's head," he said to the interpreter, drawing his revolver from the holster and taking aim. The target flickered before his eyes; fever and the wound were telling on him. Fervently he hoped the night-dew had not rusted the barrel—fortunately he kept it greased. In the wan light of dawn all eyes were fixed on the bony skull, polished clean by sunlight and the ants. Perken fired. A splash of blood showed up between the horns, spreading out towards the edges of the skull. A trickle of red stopped short, ran down suddenly on to the nose, hung on its edge, then began falling drop by drop. Timidly the chief held out his hand; a red drop hung suspended, motionless, above it; at last it fell on to his finger. He licked his

194

finger at once and uttered some words which drew the Mois' eyes, fear-stricken, towards the ground.

"Is it man's blood?" the interpreter asked.

"Yes."

Claude expected a word of explanation, but Perken was watching the Mois. Their shoulders slouched, their backs sagging and tense at once, they were huddling together; now and then a truant glance sped upwards from the group towards the skull, and furtively dropped back towards the earth. Under the intermittent scrutiny of their restless eyes, in the agonizing suspense, the splash of blood seemed growing larger with each passing second. On the upper edge it had begun to dry, but another rivulet had formed and was creeping down in lazy zigzags. The moving blood, spreading in crooked tentacles, looked like some living creature, a large red insect gripping the bluish bone in token of possession.

The chief stretched out his hand, smeared by his tongue with streaks of blood, towards the bamboo. Now Perken drank. Claude had expected a display of sudden veneration.

"They're too familiar with the supernatural," Perken explained. "They look on us as white men would regard the owner of an unusual type of gun—and fear us in much the same way. Still, we've definitely scored a point; there can be no question now of their violating the oath."

As Claude, in his turn, drank the rice-spirit he

195

could not help asking: "How did you manage it?"

"I filled one of my hollow bullets with blood from my knee."

The chief rose. Xa went off to yoke the oxen while Perken and Claude walked back to the hut, where Grabot had remained. He was lying on his side, one arm extended, his hand half open. Perken woke him and told him of the arrangements made with the Mois. Grabot sat up, his head lolling on his shoulder. He made no answer—whether from hostility or because he still was half-asleep, Claude could not judge.

"I'm convinced they will stand by the oath they've taken on the rice-spirit," Perken said to him.

Grabot opened his hand wide without replying. Claude looked away. Xa brought the carts up to the door; the guide was with him. Nothing had been stolen, and he had taken no longer than usual to yoke the oxen; the return to everyday normality, this abrupt yet casual conclusion of the tragic night, startled Claude like a reminder of the nullity of life —of his own life. No one was visible in the space below the gaur's head; at the junction of two black channels on a jagged spike of bone a drop of blood was slowly congealing, glistening in the sun.

5

With his spear the guide pointed to a Siamese village which showed as a brown patch in the forest some three hundred yards below, near a small banana-grove. It consisted of a cluster of mat huts, huddling together with their usual furtive air of creatures of the jungle. The hills rolled away to the horizon in almost parallel lines, growing lower and lower as they receded into the distance. That was Siam. The guide planted his spear in the ground to mark the spot where the exchange was to take place.

"He's chosen the place well," Claude observed. "It commands all the paths leading up to it."

Perken was lying full-length in one of the carts, as

on a stretcher. Xa had taken down the hood. Now he sat up.

"The guide's a poor damn fool! If Siam wants to take action, it'll do so after the exchange has been made. There's not the least difficulty in getting the carts which carry the jars followed. The man who follows them will guide a punitive column to the village later on."

The Moi still held his spear planted in the ground. At last he was satisfied that the white men had understood him. He turned and started back, slowly at first, then loping clumsily along like a hunted animal —a creature of the wilds homing back to its own kind, a skiff returning to its ship. Something of his presence lingered in the air after his footfalls had receded out of hearing.

Once more they were alone with their carts and the bas-reliefs, following a jungle track which led them to a village whose thatch roofs sparkled on the far side of a deep gulf of sunlight.

Some of the villagers spoke Siamese. Perken selected drivers and the journey began again with relays at each of the villages they came upon, as in Cambodia. But now they pushed ahead with haste as feverish as the pulsing of the blood in Perken's wounded leg, which was swelling larger, growing redder every day. Perken hardly ate at all and only got up when compelled to do so. Each evening his fever rose. At last they sighted the horns and tall white pinnacles of a pagoda, blue-sheened by the fierce tropical sunlight. They were approaching the first Siamese town upon their way.

They settled into the travelers' bungalow and Xa went out at once to make enquiries. There was a young native doctor who had studied at Singapore and lived most of the time in Bangkok, and an English doctor on his rounds who would be staying another couple of days. The latter was to be found, they learned, at the Chinaman's house, where he took his meals. It was just on noon.

Claude hastened to the Chinese eating-house. In a room hung with grimy mats and huge cigarette-advertisements, he discovered a white drill back, surmounted by a shock of white hair, bending below a punkah, in front of an array of soda-water bottles and greenish jars.

"You're the doctor?"

The man turned slowly, a wad of bean-sprouts poised between his lifted chop-sticks. His face was almost as white as his hair. He looked Claude up and down with an expression of ill-humored forbearance.

"Well, what's the matter *now?*"

"A white man seriously wounded. The wound is septic."

The old man placidly shrugged his shoulders and went on eating. A minute passed; at the end of his patience, Claude planted his fists firmly on the table. The doctor looked up.

"Can't you let me finish my tiffin?"

Claude fought down an impulse to box the man's

ears. Unfortunately he was the only European doctor. Claude sat down at the next table, between the man and the door.

" 'All right' would have been a shorter answer. . . . When you've done."

At last the doctor rose.

"Where's he been put?"

His tone and manner conveyed the thought: "In some damn' silly place as usual, I suppose!"

"In the bungalow."

"Come along."

The sunlight beat down on them, blinding, implacable sunlight.

No sooner had the doctor entered the room than he sat down on the bed and opened his pocket-knife, intending to slit up Perken's breeches, but the swelling had grown so enormous that Perken had already made a slit along one side. The doctor tore the drill off roughly, but his manner changed once he began examining the wound. Its gathered black head seemed to have no connection with the swollen red knee.

"Can't bend your leg, I suppose?"

"No."

"Hit by an arrow, eh?"

"I fell on a war-spike."

"How long ago?"

"Five days."

"That's bad."

"The Stiengs never poison their spikes."

"If it had been poisoned you'd be dead by now. But a man can poison himself very efficiently—his body might have been built on purpose for that!"

"I put iodine on the wound—not at once, though."

"Iodine on a deep wound like that! About as much use as saying a prayer over it!"

He ran his hand gently over the injured knee; so sensitive was it that Perken pictured the skin as thin as tissue-paper.

"A bad business. The knee-cap's loose. Pass me the thermometer. 101.8. And your temperature goes up of an evening, of course. You hardly eat anything, eh?"

"No."

"So you've been traveling amongst the Stiengs!"

The doctor shrugged his shoulders again, and seemed lost in thought. Then he looked at Perken once more, vindictively.

"Why couldn't you keep quiet?" he exclaimed.

Perken cast a keen glance at the man's bloodless face.

"When an opium-smoker starts preaching about 'keeping quiet,'" he said, "I always advise him to go and lie down. If it's the time for you to have your pipe, go away and smoke it and come back later. It'll be pleasanter all round that way!"

"I'm not asking your advice!"

"You've heard of Perken, haven't you?"

"What the hell . . . ?"

"Well, I'm Perken. In other words, I warn you to look out."

"When one considers how simple it is to have a quiet life . . . !"

Once more he bent over the wound, not out of compunction, it seemed, but as if he were looking for something. He was following up his thoughts. "Folly!" he muttered. "Damned folly!" A faint, disillusioned smile hovered on his lips; it did not lift the corners of his mouth, but dragged them down. The smile flickered slowly out, came back again.

"So you're Perken, are you?"

"No, I'm the Shah of Persia!"

"And you think it's a fine thing, don't you, to have made your mark in this part of the world, to have led a strenuous life, kept moving, instead of keeping quiet, quite quiet . . . ?"

"Have I asked you to expound the advantages of keeping 'quite quiet,' as you put it?"

The smile vanished once more.

"Well, Mr. Perken, this is how things stand. You're suffering from septic arthritis of the knee. In less than a fortnight you'll be dead. And there's nothing to be done about it, let me tell you. Not a damned thing!"

Perken's first impulse was to strike the man, but there had been little animosity, only a world of bitterness, in his voice, and he controlled the movement. He realized that here was simply another instance of the confirmed opium-smoker's distaste for every form of action.

"Well, we'll have to look for a doctor who takes his job seriously," Claude said.

"You don't believe me?"

Perken pondered deeply before replying.

"Before you came I had a feeling that that was very likely how things were. . . . I've often rubbed shoulders with death."

"I've heard that sort of stuff before. Cut it out!"

"Still . . . I'm not convinced."

"You're wrong. There's nothing to be done. Nothing. Smoke, and you'll have some peace, and not be bothered by unpleasant thoughts. The opium's pretty good in these parts. Whenever the pain gets unbearable, give yourself an injection, anyhow. I'll lend you one of my needles. You don't dope?"

"No."

"Of course not! In that case, you've only got to administer three times the normal dose, to finish things off whenever you feel like it. Your boy can come with me to get the needle."

"I've been wounded by war-spikes before."

"Not in the knee. The toxins forming in it will poison you slowly. There's only one way out, and that is amputation. But you haven't got time to go to a town where they could operate. Just give yourself the injections and try to think of something else. And keep quiet. It'll be a pleasant change for you. . . . That's all."

"What about lancing the wound?"

"I couldn't get anywhere. The infection is far too deep-seated, and it's protected by the bone. But, if you prefer, call in the Siamese doctor, as this youngster here proposes. I must warn you that he has no clinical experience. And he's a native. But I shouldn't be surprised if you prefer a native to a white doctor."

"Just at the moment, very much!"

As he was leaving the room, the doctor turned and looked once more at Perken and Claude.

"Nothing the matter with you, young man?"

"No."

"Because, while I'm about it . . ."

But it was on Perken that his eyes were fixed. His heavy stare and knitted brows gave the impression that something hovered in the background of his thoughts, like a reflection in a misted mirror. . . . At last he turned and left the room.

"A pity that a hard smack on the face has so little meaning in these parts," Claude said. "A charming specimen of humanity, isn't he? Shall I fetch the Siamese doctor?"

"Yes, at once, please. A white doctor touring in this district was bound to be a queer specimen anyhow— rotten with dope . . . or women. Xa, go and fetch the local Station Officer. Show him this." He handed the boy an official-looking document, on which his name alone was written in Roman characters. "Tell him it comes from Perken. And get me some women for to-night."

When Claude returned—the native doctor was to follow him up immediately—the Station Officer was already there. Perken and he were talking in Siamese. The official listened, gave brief answers and took some notes. Then he wrote a dozen sentences or so at Perken's dictation.

"Well, what about Grabot?" Claude asked, as soon as the officer had gone.

"We'll get him. That fellow believes, as I do, that the Siamese government will snap at the opportunity of sending out a punitive expedition and occupying as much territory as possible in the independent tract. A first-rate pretext, and everything to gain. As a white man has been tortured the French can't raise objections; they might want to use a similar excuse themselves one day—which would be a pity. What's more, the people who've got the railroad concession are keen as mustard on a military occupation. . . . He took down my telegram. We should get a reply to-night. If the expeditionary column starts by blowing up a village there'll be a general panic throughout the region."

The mat that served as window was slightly raised and Claude could see the road. It was empty. Would that Siamese doctor never come? The palm-trees dissolved into a sky of incandescent blue, shimmering like the light in vacuum-tubes. The sun beat on the ground with such intensity that all life seemed paralysed. Here was not the stifling languor of the jungle, but an aggressive heat, a savage force that little by little subjected earth and men to its implacable dominion. No thought, no scheme, no effort of the will but crumbled into dust, volatilized into the fiery air. Into the silent room the heat poured wave on wave, and now another presence rose with it from the white-hot earth and sleeping animals, and from the torpid bodies of the two men lying in the sweltering twilight: the presence of death. So long as the English doctor had been there Perken had been minded to answer back, rather than try to understand. And, after that, he had forced himself to act, postponing the return of a thought which, like the blazing sunlight, loomed on the threshold of his consciousness. But now at last he must confront it, face to face.

The doctor, for all his cool assertiveness, had not convinced him and, despite what he had said about them at the time, his own sensations, now that he set to analysing them rigorously, did not convince him either. He was familiar with wounds. Fever of this kind and the recurrent agony that racked his knee were not new to him. It seemed to him that the cause of his trouble lay in the sensitiveness of the abscess, in the reflexes which made the swollen flesh wince from contact with even the lightest object—rather than in any form of blood-poisoning; of that he could detect no symptom. Against this direct assurance, vouched for by the wound itself, there was only a human—and fallible—opinion. He had a strange conviction that he could wrest a reprieve from the Siamese doctor, by dint of efforts.

But hardly had the man entered the room than the fabric of his hope collapsed with the abruptness of a rude awakening. The man's professional indifference was, in itself, enough to lay in ruins all the self-defensive world he had set up. And now it seemed to Perken that he was being wrenched away from his body, that irresponsible body of his, intent on leading him to death. The Siamese doctor removed the dressing and, squatting in native fashion beside the bed, proceeded to examine the wound. Perken recapitulated the symptoms he had already described to the English doctor. Without replying, the Siamese continued palpating the wound with skilful fingers. For all his burning impatience Perken felt no distress. Once more he had an overt enemy to face, were that enemy none other than his flesh and blood.

"Mr Perken, on my way here I met Dr Blackhouse. As a man he may be . . . unworthy, but he is an experienced physician. He informed me in his condescending English way—as if I could not possibly know about such a disease!—that what you have is septic arthritis. I have read about it in my textbooks, though so far I have not come across such a case. You have all the symptoms. The only way to deal with a disease of this nature is amputation. But, in the present deplorable state of medical science in this part of the world—"

Perken lifted his hand to cut short the harangue. The man's Europeanized gabble recalled to him the fact that this tactful confirmation of the sentence of death passed on him was being enounced in view of suitable remuneration. Paid, the doctor took his leave. Perken watched his going—as if it were a final proof.

He felt less sure of death than of its menace, for he was at once bound to his body and detached from it, like the criminals of old time who were condemned to death by drowning, tied to a corpse. Within him death lay in wait, but so alien, so apart from him it seemed, that once again he felt a fight impending. But then a look from Claude brought him back to his body, to himself. It was a look of deep understanding, of perfect fellowship, in which the fervent confraternity of courage and compassion intensified the vital unity of all living flesh in the presence of death's victim. Though Perken clung to Claude more than to any other human being, he now felt as if it were Claude who decreed his death. More convincing than the doctor's words, Claude's involuntarily lowered eyelids forced on his consciousness the unappealable decision. The twinges in his knee returned, accompanied by spasms that made the leg contract. Pain and death, he reflected, work in concert; one is the never-failing herald of the other. Then the wave of agony ebbed, and with it passed the mental effort he had made against it. Now only a dull ache persisted, like a crouching beast about to spring. For the first time in his life a force far stronger than his own had entrenched itself within him, a force against which all hope was hopeless. Nevertheless, against that force he must put up a fight.

"What's so queer, Claude, about death's approach, even when it's . . . fairly remote, is that one knows all of a sudden all one wants, knows it quite definitely, once for all. . . ."

They gazed at each other, held by the bond of silence which had already more than once united them. Perken was sitting on his bed with his leg stretched out. His eyes had grown clear again, but in them was a pensive look, as if his will had not yet risen clear of past regrets. Claude wondered what thoughts lay behind that look.

"Do you want to go with the column?"

Perken was taken by surprise; no such idea had crossed his mind. The Stiengs, to his thinking, had no part in his death.

"No. What I need now is—men. I must go back to my own country."

Suddenly Claude realized how much the older of the two Perken was. The difference was not apparent in his face or voice. But now it seemed that all the years of Perken's life weighed on him like an inveterate faith; yes, he and Perken were utterly unlike, men of alien races.

209

"What about the stones?"

"That's hardest of all to bear just now—frustrated hope!"

Claude reflected. Could Perken, alone, make the arduous journey to his mountains?

There was nothing now to prevent Claude from going straight to Bangkok. Nothing . . . except death's imminence.

"I'll come with you," he said.

There was a long silence. Such rare moments of intense communion bring a feeling of constraint and, as though to shake it off, both men turned towards the window. The white glare shimmering beneath the window-matting dazzled their eyes; the passing minutes seemed to melt into the furnace of the sunlight. Claude's thoughts strayed back to the stones piled on the carts, and now they seemed lifeless, inert things, drained of all the violent hostility which had animated them. If he left them at the outpost would they still be there when he got back? And if not—? "Why did I decide to go with him?" he asked himself. But no, he could not desert Perken; to do that would be to abandon him not only to the world of men from which he felt himself irrevocably severed, but to death as well. The strength of their fellow-feeling, unsuspected until now, struck him as a revelation. And was it not by sudden resolutions of this kind, and by them alone, that he could foster the contempt which separated him from the conventions and compromises of the herd? He was risking much, but whether he won through or lost, he could but gain in hardihood by the venture, and sate his thirst for courage, his deep awareness of the world's futility and human wretchedness. Thus, though less consciously, had his grandfather thought and felt. . . . Suddenly the screen across the doorway moved aside, flooding the room with dancing flakes of light. And all his arguments, his self-communings, were dust before a fiery wind, trivial things of no account; all he would ever really know about himself, it seemed, was—what he wanted!

A bare-footed native handed Perken a telegram, the preliminary instructions given to the officer in charge of the station. *"Arrange billets locally for base of operations punitive expedition eight hundred men machine-guns."*

"Eight hundred men," Perken repeated. "That means they're going to subdue the whole district. How far will they go? Even if I hadn't made up my mind, that would settle it; I'll have to go up country. And *they*—damn them!—have machine-guns."

Xa came in.

"Master, velly fine women getting."

"Can find some for me too?" Claude asked.

"Can find."

They went to the door.

Two women were standing on the right of the threshold. For one of them, the smaller of the two, a girl with soft ripe lips and flowers in her hair, Perken felt an immediate distaste. He was in no mood

211

for languor. He beckoned to the other without so much as a glance at her. The smaller girl went away.

The air of the room hung motionless as if time stood still, and the tense silence in which, save Perken's trembling fingers, nothing seemed alive, was dominated by the woman's face, a face of Asiatic impassivity, with an aquiline, finely modeled nose. It was not desire that made him tremble, nor was it his fever, though from the preternatural intensity of his vision he knew his fever must be rising. He trembled as a gambler trembles. Not that on this occasion he had any fear of impotence; but, despite the heady perfume of the woman's body, flooding his senses, his mind was in a ferment of apprehension.

She lay down, naked, her sleek, hairless body dim in the half-light; only the faint line between her thighs, and her eyes showed clearly. It was upon her eyes he fixed his gaze, seeking, as he had so often sought in vain, some hint of the insidious shame of nudity. To escape the spell which his inexplicable feelings were casting on her, she shut her eyes. Man's desire was no new thing to her, but in the atmosphere of the room, the utter silence, and in his scrutiny, there was something that worked on her imagination. She waited. The position of the cushions compelled her slightly to relax her arms and legs, and lying thus, with half-parted lips, she seemed to be kindling within herself the ardor of her own desire, seeking its satisfaction by a gentle heaving of her breasts. In a slow, persistent rhythm they rose and fell, a rhythm that, though unchanged, was ever gaining in intensity, till the whole room seemed pervaded by their movement. Like a spent wave they sank, and slowly rose again, the muscles growing taut, the pools of shadow deepening round them. When, helped by her, he put his arms around her, he knew her fear of him was passing. She let one hip take her weight, so as slightly to change her posture. For an instant a ray of yellow-golden light, keen as a whip-lash, flickered across her back, vanished between her legs. The soft warmth of her body flooded his senses. Suddenly, she bit her lip; a little, wilful gesture that bore witness to her inability to subdue the heaving of her breasts.

He scanned her face and bluish eyelids as though they were a mask. His face was only a few inches from hers, but he felt as if the blind desire linking his body with this woman's were another's; he possessed it as he might have struck it. The whole of her face, the whole woman, was concentrated in her uplifted mouth. Suddenly her fleshy lips began to quiver, curled back across her teeth, and, as if here had been its starting-point, a long spasm shuddered down her body that had till now been stiff, inhuman, motionless as a sun-scared tree under the fires of noon. But for her mouth her face might have been a dead woman's, though in response to each of Perken's movements her finger-nail gritted on the sheet. As the tide of passion rose, her finger ceased to touch the bed and halted in mid-air. Her eyes were tightly

213

closed. Now her mouth closed, too; only the corners of her lips continued twitching. Frenzied with self-centered passion, her body was withdrawing itself from him irrevocably. Never, never would he apprehend, never share, this woman's sensations; never could the frenzy which thrilled her body be for him anything but a proof of the unbridgeable gulf between them. Without love there can be no possession. Carried away by forces he could not control, unable even to make her realize his presence by tearing himself away from her, he too closed his eyes, thrown back upon himself as on a noxious drug, drunk with a wild desire violently to crush out of existence this stranger's face that urged him on to death.

Part Four

1

More nights passed and more days, with death, like Claude, ever at Perken's side; days and nights of torment from mosquitoes and the heat that seemed to well up from his throbbing knee. In these vast forests day and night moved to an incalculable rhythm—the alternation of the clearings, tracts of daylight hewn out of the jungle, with the green darkness of the close-meshed trees. Here night seemed, like the viscous leaves, inordinately lengthened; time itself was rotten with decay. Then, for a while, the open clearings came at shorter intervals, as though at last the forest were retreating, yielding to the daylight. But Perken knew better—he knew that this was only a wide valley; further on another sea of jungle would beat upon his rigid body and his enfeebled will; and all his hopes seemed wilting, evaporating, under the wildfire of the stinging insects, amid the baying of the jungle dogs.

He had the boy remove his shoe for a moment; the skin was an angry red, stippled with insect-bites as if it had been tattooed. Across his pain and the burning of his skin, amid the general corruption, the endless clamor of the monkeys, and the twisted boughs that now they were advancing into Laos and his territory they encountered at every break in the forest, the furtive, unseen presence of the Stiengs, like a miasma of decay, infested every cranny of the jungle. Now that the jars had been made over, and Grabot given up and sent to Bangkok Hospital, the punitive column, taking along with it the men who had been injured on the way by spikes and man-traps, had marched into the village, dynamited the entrance-gate and cleaned up the huts with hand-grenades. The village was now a charnel-house, given up to the black pigs rooting amongst the shards of broken jars for bellies black with vermin. In their stampede across the jungle the Stiengs looted all the villages they came upon, and the pursuing column lost many men on the way, chiefly through septic wounds. The native levies treated the sick abandoned by the fugitives with bombs, and dispatched the wounded with their bayonets. The migrant tribes streamed through the forest like a herd of animals pressing on to the last water-pools in a time of drouth; nothing upon the undulating canopy of leaves betrayed their daylong march towards the East, but, at each nightfall, straight columns of smoke rose high into the stagnant air, marking above the limitless expanse of trees their nightly camping-place.

Some days after Claude and Perken had left the Siamese outpost, they had begun to see these fires, and, the further they advanced towards the tract where Perken had established himself and the area of railway construction, the more numerous became the pillars of smoke; at every break in the forest they could now be seen strung out along the horizon. Close behind them, in the darkness murmurous with cicadas, was the column, and behind the column was the Siamese government. "Men of my sort should always have the forces of a State to play with," Perken had once remarked. And somewhere yonder, behind a wall of darkness, the forces of a State were on the march, scattering in flight before them the wild life of the jungle—soon to be followed by its human denizens as well—pushing on mile by mile their rail-head, burying year by year a little further on the corpses of their pioneers. By daylight the pillars of smoke rose clean-cut as tree-trunks and, with the aid of field-glasses, red-dyed skulls could be made out between them, silhouetted against the sky. In the vast spaces of the forest the crackling of the distant fires seemed stifled by a pall of silence. When, Claude wondered, would the advancing smoke-signals strike across the trail that they were following? As, with the night, the smoke-cloud dissolved into the darkness, a searchlight at the apex of the railroad raked the zenith; it seemed as if the great migration of the Mois, moving like a driven flock towards new pasturage under cover of the leaves, pivoted on the luminous triangle projected by the white men on the sky.

Across another opening in the forest a low-lying tract of country was coming into view, spread out below them like a landscape seen from an airplane; with its rolling contours and vistas fading out into a haze of deepest blue it seemed another world, remote from the path which they were following. Claude pictured the sunlight shimmering down there as on the surface of a lake—a glassy sheen upon the foothills, a mist of golden spray around the palm-groves. Further on some white Buddhist pagodas showed up against a dark mass of vegetation, the precincts of Samrong village, which marked the frontier of Perken's territory, the first of the allied Lao villages and the first one where he knew the chief. In front of them the smoke soared up into the empty dome of sky, making its vastness vaster still; the progress of the fires was so intimately linked up with the life of the forest that it, too, seemed invincible, the handiwork of nature, of the earth, and not of men—like an eruption or a rising tide.

Perken was puzzled. "Why the devil should they be advancing on a village where the warriors are armed? There must be some compulsion behind it."

"Hunger, perhaps," Claude suggested.

"Anyhow the column has lost touch with them by now; the orders were that it was not to cross the river. Across the river it's Savan's territory; mine lies immediately beyond."

Under their eyes the river wound in a hairpin bend; its surface shone like incandescent steel, the only touch of whiteness in the blue gulf below.

"I'll have to help Savan to defend his village."

"What? In your present state . . . ?"

"If we follow the mountain-crest we should get there well before they do. Or one day later, at most."

He kept his eyes fixed on the village and the forest, but, though he was gnawing his nails to the quick to keep himself from scratching, his gaze grew blurred, unsteady. Claude knew too well the depth of the allegiance which drew him thither, to insist. Moreover, a new anxiety kept him from speaking; a persistent sound of blows like hammer-strokes was throbbing faintly in the languid silence, and in his mind it somehow linked itself with the tall smoke-wraiths advancing in an interminable procession, like phantoms of the forest, along the line of the horizon. Too weak to fill that vast abyss of light, the sounds were swallowed up in it like the rare birds which, rising for a moment from the dark mass of trees, dropped back at once into the leaves like falling stones, stunned by the furious impact of the sun. The regular intervals between these sounds, merged in the universal light, invested them with a strange ritual significance, like warning drumbeats on a distant planet. Claude recalled the clang of his claw-hammer on the stone.

"Listen!"

"What . . . ?"

Perken had heard only the cadence of his pain. Now he held his breath. One. Two. Three. Four. The blows came faster, distinct from each other, but muffled; soft, flabby thuds. The slow advance of the fires stressed their acceleration.

"Men at work somewhere," Claude observed. "Do you think they're digging themselves in?"

"Who? The Mois? No, it can't be they. Their fires are moving ahead all the time, and that noise is much nearer us."

Perken tried to locate the origin of the sound with his field-glasses, but without success. The bluish heat-haze, though it did not hide the forest, made outlines indistinct. Each throb of agony in his knee jarred through his body like a jangling bell, yet never quite in rhythm with the distant thudding. There was no sign of human presence, and it seemed as if the inexplicable hammering, the smoke-wraiths, were nature's work alone—symbols of her enmity.

Suddenly, in the distance, a speck of dazzling light flashed into view, like a window-pane struck by a sunbeam. Raising his glasses again, Perken had the cart stop, and examined it carefully. There was no water thereabouts, that he knew. His foot, inert and yet alive with pain, was between him and the point of light, but its dark mass seemed independent of him—it was as if he suffered in another's flesh—and he made no effort to move it away. He sat up instead, and now he had a clearer view. Claude held out his hand, but Perken did not pass him the field-glasses. The speck of light rose and fell in a steady rhythm, like the sound of hammering which seemed to issue from it. Perken lowered his hand and Claude made another attempt to get the glasses, which Perken was gripping tightly; at last he gave them up.

"Still—that's the river down there, isn't it?" he said.

Claude fixed his eyes on the spot of light; it was far *beyond* the river, and looked like a cooking-pot or some other camp utensil. Close beside it he made out some human forms, some slender objects stacked criss-cross, and some larger surfaces forming geometrical patterns. These last he recognized at once as tents. And the criss-cross lines were piles of rifles. He looked back to the river; yes, it was far behind the camp—miles, perhaps, behind it. Then another speck of light flashed up in front of the first one, in the direction of the Mois' fires.

"Is that the column?" Claude asked.

Perken was silent for a while. At last he spoke.

"For them, too. . . . I'm a dead man!"

Misted with horror, his eyes strayed from his leg towards the moving points of light, and back again. At last he ceased gazing at his leg. The strokes of the wooden mallets driving in tent-pegs had a hollow resonance—it was as if they fell on empty casks—that, as the waves of sound spread slowly out upon the air, engulfed the smoke-wraiths, even the vast forest— all the cowering kingdom of the sunlight. Man's will had come into its own, taken command again . . . in the service of death. Despite his pain Perken felt furiously alive, up in arms against this affirmation of his failure. . . . No, there was fight in him yet! Nevertheless, all he had achieved lay dead before his eyes—like his own corpse; in less than a week the column well might reach his territory, all his life's work be proved a vain endeavor.

He looked at the piled rifles. The column was advancing, ignoring the wide loop of the river whence rose a phosphorescent sheen, shot with flashes of electric blue. He looked at the tents. Yet he felt no certitude about it all, only a sickening suspense like the partial loss of consciousness that precedes a bout of vomiting. Involuntarily all his attention reverted to his pain, rising and falling like a ship at sea; and only in its lulls did he regain awareness of the progress of the column and of death, working in concert, marching steadily towards their goal like the long trail of smoking fires.

"I shouldn't be surprised," he thought, "if making good in death doesn't mean more for me than making good in life. . . ."

Once more he brought his glasses to bear on the village; between the two dark blurs of his shoes it showed up with extraordinary clearness. His life was falling steeply into an abyss, and on its crumbling verge that village stood out like a rock, a solid something he must cling to, and, clinging, grapple with, as he had grappled with the sculptures of the temple. The field-glasses strayed back—of their own will, it seemed—towards the column. But the two waves were following, one on the other, and it would be the Stiengs whom he must tackle first.

"We'll reach Savan's village, too, a good while before they get there."

"This man Savan—is he to be trusted . . . absolutely?"

"No. I can really trust only the chiefs in the north. But—we've no choice. . . ."

2

But for one spot, a patch of inky blackness, Samrong and its Buddhist temples were ringed in on all sides by rapid firing, ever growing in intensity, a rapid crackling of reports and echoes. Prisoned within the circle, brooded the sultry languor of the Lao night, humming with cicadas, lit by the red glow of a beacon-fire.

"Still nothing in sight down there, Claude?" Perken asked. He could no longer sit up. Claude picked up the glasses again.

"I can't see a thing. . . ."

Before he had put the glasses down there was the flash of another shot, this time near the summit of a hill. The echo followed on, a full tone higher than the report itself. Another shot flashed out, dingy beside the brightness of the stars.

"Do you think the Stiengs have surrounded the village?"

"Out of the question." Perken pointed to the dim outline of a hill. "Our scouts haven't opened fire over there. That means they're not trying to advance."

"Mois knowing machine-guns over by railhead," Xa observed.

Beyond the zone of rifle-fire pink tongues of flame, the Mois' camp-fires, flickered. Perken kept his eyes fixed on them; for their presence meant that the column had not yet advanced so far. A moving form crossed the field of the glasses, quite near, blotting out his objective.

"Who goes there?"

The floor of the hut stood on wooden piles and from where he was lying Perken overlooked the compound. The dark form vanished. Without aiming, Perken fired in its direction, and waited to hear a cry. Nothing came.

"That's the second time. . . ."

"Ever since you advised them to hold up the column," Claude said, "things have been going wrong. So long as it was only a matter of helping the village to resist the Stiengs . . ."

"Damned idiots!"

The scouts posted by Perken were firing much more frequently. The horde of Stiengs which the column had driven before it was evidently pressing on towards the village.

"Are you sure the advice you've given them was sound? Personally, I'm afraid that, if they send men forward to parley, the leader of the column will tell them to go to the devil, and, if they fire, the machine-guns will be turned on them."

"The instructions given to the column don't admit of fighting them. They are Buddhists, peaceful folk. And they're no better armed than my men are. No, there'll be parleying all right. But if once they let the Siamese levies get in without first making terms, an 'administration,' as the Siamese call it, is bound to ensue. Savan's the only one to understand that—but his authority as chief is getting nearly as shaky as those marksmen's trigger-fingers! There can be no doubt about it; if once they get in here, the way will then lie open right up to my country. . . . But it's only the chiefs up north I've got a real hold on."

The wild fragrance of the fires drifted past them on the darkness.

"It isn't merely to organize their resistance to the Stiengs that we're stopping here," he added.

The firing was steadily growing more rapid, and its rhythm—like slow machine-gun fire—worked on Perken's nerves. The rattle of musketry came and went in fitful gusts, contrasting with the steady glow of the Stiengs' fires. New fires flared up. As the bar-rage of rifle-fire grew more intense, they rose, remote and stationary, several rows deep. Against the intermittent flashes of the guns their immobility was so impressive as to make them seem irrelevant to the fighting, natural emanations of the heat and the dark forest.

"Do you think they can get together for a mass attack?" Claude asked. "There are quite a lot of them, you know. Look at their fires!"

Perken reflected for a moment.

"They could certainly rush the village if they did. But they haven't got it in them to join forces. My men, and the chiefs whom I've been urging to coöperate, are Laos and Buddhists—like these people here—and it's all I can do to hold even them together. And don't forget the Stiengs always attack a *moving* enemy; that's how they're built. It isn't easy to launch an attack when old corpses are lying all around you, or to concert one when the air is stinking with them! No, the driving force behind them just now is principally hunger. To-morrow the column will be at their heels again." After a moment's pause he added: "And at ours, too."

The firing broke out anew and soon died down again—a wave of sound rising and falling above the fires. A man emerged from the shadows round the entrance of the hut; his bare feet gripped the rungs of the ladder soundlessly, like hands. Successively his head, his chest and legs showed up in the dim radiance of the lamplight. A messenger. Perken sat up, wincing with pain, and sank back again. So overpowering was each sudden surge of agony that, whenever he had an order to impart, he waited for its lull, as if he were awaiting the departure of an intruder. The man had begun speaking, hurriedly, in short sentences—like a schoolboy repeating a lesson. Claude guessed that he had learned by heart the Siamese phrases he employed; he watched Perken's face, and not the native's, as if the silence of a European must be, of the two, the more understandable. Perken had ceased looking at the man, though the latter went on speaking. Perken's eyes were shut and, but for the faint quivering of his cheeks, he might have been asleep. Suddenly he looked up.

"What is it?" Claude asked.

"He says that the Stiengs know I'm here; that's why they made the first attack and are coming on again. And, of course, we're less dangerous opponents than the column."

The firing had stopped. The messenger went away, accompanied by Xa.

"Anyhow it's impossible to surround the village. And, what's more, we have rifles."

Two shots, a two-fold echo, jarred the air, followed again by silence.

"He told me," Perken continued, "something else. Some of the railway engineers are with the column."

Claude was beginning to see daylight.

"But they're going strong at it over there. Why, they touched off at least a dozen mines to-day!"

"And each of those damned explosions," Perken said, "was another rap on the knuckles for me!

They're pushing ahead, no doubt of it. If they come this way . . ."

"But surely they wouldn't change the lay-out of their line at this stage?"

Perken stared into the darkness. "It would save them a great deal of money, of course, taking the line across my territory. And I expect they're feeling very bucked up just now, game for anything—with the Mois scattering before them like sheep. But they'll be up against it if they come *my* way, column or no column!"

Claude did not reply.

"Column or no column," Perken repeated.

Still Claude made no comment.

"Yes," Perken went on, "with three machine-guns, with only three machine-guns I could have held them up."

There was an outburst of desultory firing, which soon died away.

"They're going to lay off for a while. Here is the dawn."

"Wasn't Savan to come at sunrise?"

"I believe so. . . . Oh, the fools, the God-damned fools—if they let the column through!"

3

The day was breaking as Savan climbed the ladder.
How many dawns would rise again before—the
end? As the old chief rose into view, framed in the
doorway, Perken gazed curiously at his stubbly gray
hair, his nose—the nose of a Lao Buddha—and his
shifty eyes. Since death had lodged itself within him,
all living things had lost their individual forms for
Perken. He knew this chief personally, and yet he
seemed less real than the old savage in the Stieng village. Only one thing about Savan caught his attention—his hands itching for a palaver. An old fellow
good for talk, and little else! Other heads appeared,
one above the other; the chief had brought his fol-
lowers with him. They all came in. Savan hesitated.

232

When he was with white men he did not care to squat, and he loathed sitting on a chair. So he remained standing, eyes studiously lowered, saying nothing. That Asiatic habit of preposterous silence always irritated Claude. Perken was used to it, but, now he was wounded, suffered it less patiently. Such periods of suspense brought cruelly home to him his incapacity to move. He was the first to speak.

"If the column comes this way, you know what will happen, don't you?"

The hillsides dropping away towards the far horizon were growing faintly visible. A few hundred yards off some skulls tied to isolated trees peered through the dusk. A morning wind ruffled the nearer tree-tops, and the great sea of vegetation sweeping from hill to hill, stirred by the tribesmen in their invisible retreat, seemed to carry on the movement. A mine exploded. The railhead lay behind the hut and they could not see the blasting operations, but no sooner had the last low rumble died across the valley than they heard the clatter of stones and rocky masses hurtling down.

"The column will be here the day after to-morrow. I tell you again—if your village puts up a fight, with the firearms you've got, it will turn off and go north. Otherwise the railroad will come here. Do you want to be at the beck and call of Siamese officials?"

Savan made a negative—but obviously mistrustful—gesture.

"It's easier to fight against a flying column which
233

has no orders to attack you than against regular troops sent up here by the railroad."

Turning to Claude, he added in French: "But by then, perhaps, I shall be dead!"

Yet, amazingly, the tone of his voice belied the words; faith in his life had returned to him.

Some natives came in one by one, and squatted on the floor of the hut. They began talking, but not in Siamese, and Perken did not know their dialect; their hostility, nevertheless, was unmistakable. Savan pointed towards them.

"To begin with, they are afraid of the Stiengs."

"For men armed with rifles the Stiengs don't exist!"

The chief's finger, poised in mid-air, veered round towards the forest. Perken examined the foliage through his glasses. Spear-shafts capped with roughly-shaped balls were being slowly hoisted to the summits of the tallest trees. The Stiengs were no longer in flight. Failing fetishes, their supply of which was small, a fantastic medley of skulls and animals slain in the chase was springing up out of the forest, flaunting its barbaric menace against the morning sky. It looked as if a litter of dry bones, the progeny of the great gaur's skull, had swarmed down to the river's edge, and the river, too, were fleeing before a plague of monstrous insects. Ribs and skulls, and even snakeskins, bleached white as chalk, were swaying in the morning breeze—a grotesque avowal of

234

the famine that was devastating the migrant tribes. To the right, quite near the river, was a fetish which portrayed a woman mourning her dead with a haunting pathos quite unknown to civilization. Above it was a human skull set off with little feathers. Perken put down his glasses. More natives had come into the hut. Two of them had rifles that glinted in the dim light. Something in the scene brought back to him the hut where Grabot's jacket had hung.

"You are risking your lives, the lives of all. If you send envoys to parley, and fire on the column, it won't push on. I know what its orders are. And it can take the Stiengs in the rear. Otherwise—"

Several of the natives present understood Siamese. A chorus of excited protests, like the yelping of a pack of dogs, cut short his phrase. After a moment's hesitation Savan spoke.

"They say that you're to blame for the Stiengs' attack on us."

"They're attacking you because they are starving."

All the men fixed their eyes on Savan who, yet again, hesitated before continuing.

"They say that if you weren't here the Stiengs would leave us in peace."

Perken's only answer was a shrug of his shoulders.

"And," the chief added, "they want you to go away."

Perken banged his bed angrily with his fist. All

the squatting natives sprang up like startled frogs. The two men armed with rifles leveled them at the whites.

"That's done it!" Claude said to himself. "It was madness!"

Perken's eyes seemed fixed on something or someone behind the threatening faces. Xa, however, was not in the hut.

"If they move," he shouted, his eyes still fixed on a point behind them, "Shoot!"

Without lowering their rifles the two men glanced behind them, over their shoulders. Two shots rang out. Perken had fired through his pocket. So painful was the recoil that he fancied for a moment he had fired into his knee. But one of the Laos was tottering. The other remained standing, but had dropped his rifle and was pawing his belly with both hands, his mouth agape, his eyes glazed with the blank bewilderment of death. In the general scramble to get away, he, too, began to totter, his outstretched fingers sawing the air above the heads of those in flight. The padding of bare feet died out into a profound silence.

Only Savan remained in the hut.

"And now?" he said to Perken.

He was awaiting with resignation the disasters which the white man's madness brings ineluctably, sooner or later, in its train. The world of Buddhism and resigned indifference in which he had his being seemed incarnate in him now. The two bodies lay on

236

the floor, curled up like animals asleep, the blood gushing from them without a sound. He stood beside them, motionless as a phantom, gazing with unseeing eyes towards the compound where no one now was visible. "Those fellows who spoke up like that just now," Perken reflected, "must have been his rivals. I expect he's not at all sorry to be rid of them." Suddenly he caught sight of the bodies lying just in front of him, the blood of each still trickling from an unseen orifice as from something that had never been alive. Though he knew that they were there, he was haunted by a notion they had fled along with the others. Well, they were dead. And he? Was he still alive? Or dying? What, he wondered, would ensure Savan's coöperation? Interest and compulsion—obviously. Yes, these men could be persuaded to take action; but for that there must be the revolution or the war he had been planning for so many years. Had Savan consented to put up a fight against the column, half the village would have fled, most likely. In a flash of understanding he knew that all the alliances which once had seemed to promise so much—to give his life a meaning—were precarious, no more dependable than this vacillating chief by whose side he had never fought. Against an invasion by the whites, against the column, against the mines that thundered in the valley, he could only count on the help of men with whom he was united by a human bond, on men who had a sense of loyalty, on his own men. And even they . . . But, had he not been wounded, the Laos would never have dared to level their guns at him. Well, they might think him "done for," but, in his own eyes, he was nothing of the sort —as yet. Hadn't he shown those two dead men as much? Raising his eyes, he looked at Savan. As their eyes met he saw, as if the chief had said so in as many words, that he looked on him as a dying man. For the second time he saw his death reflected in another's eye. A wild desire came over him to shoot the man down—as if murder, and nothing else, could enable him to assert his existence, stave off the imminence of death. That selfsame look, he was to see it now in all men's eyes. His frenzied impulse to take death by the throat as if it were a beast of prey, and grapple with it, the impulse which had urged him to shoot Savan, was beating on his mind's defenses like a wave of madness. Henceforward in the thoughts of all his men he would have his bitterest foe—the knowledge of his downfall—to contend with. He remembered an uncle of his, a Danish squire, who after a life of wild extravagances, in his last agony, had summoned up all his will-power to repress the cries of pain his tortured nerves were wringing from him, and fought resolutely back the hideous terror that convulsed his shoulders like an ague. According to his last wishes he had been given the burial of a Hun king, mounted on his dead horse shored up by stakes. . . .

"Yes, I must be going."

238

4

Now there were no more villages on their way; the first spurs of the mountains whence Perken hoped for succor fretted the skyline; the river lay below them. Skimming the surface of the jungle, birds passed in heavy flight, butterflies glinted to and fro. And, fleeing from the Mois, whom the column was driving on and on before it, a multitude of tiny animals, monkeys for the most part, scampered away in panic as before a forest fire. They crossed the river in their hundreds, like flurries of dry leaves as they approached it, like tom-cats when they halted on the bank, their tails in air. Perched on a hidden boulder, a big monkey was gesticulating in mid-stream; through the glasses, Claude observed his antics. He looked like a drenched dog and was busily plucking off the tiny monkeys clinging for dear life upon his back. Once they had made the further bank, the monkeys vanished like a puff of smoke across the creaking branches. His glimpses of their passage between the banks of jungle linked in Claude's mind the reach of dazzling water with the vast tidal refluence of the migrant tribes.

The fires, that now kept blazing up throughout the day, stretched thin veils of smoke along the hillside; even the sunlight of high noon did not abate them. Little by little they progressed along the middle slopes, like a stealthy, soft-footed army on the march, advancing through the windless air towards the track the white men followed. The smoke of each new-kindled fire, nearer and more menacing than its precursor, rose straight and thick into the air, dilating to a plume that, slowly evanescent, merged into the shroud of smoke that swathed the hillside. His eyes intent upon the middle distance, watching the rising shafts of smoke, each like another bolt shot home to bar their progress, Claude felt his apprehension gaining on him.

"There's another fire shooting up," he said. "One more of them, and we shan't get through!"

But Perken did not open his eyes.

"There are moments," he murmured, as if he were talking to himself, "when I feel the whole damned business hasn't the least importance."

"Our being cut off, you mean?"

"No. Death."

Beyond the mountains lay Perken's territory, by them defended, pent in the solitude of its unbeaconed crags. On the other side was the railroad. Did Perken die, Claude would be thrown back on the bas-reliefs awaiting him down there; unaided, the Stiengs would never dare to launch an attack against the railway line.

Perken was sinking into a state of torpor. Close to his ears humming mosquitoes wove their tracery of subtle sounds, spreading a tingling mesh of tiny stabs upon the deep-set throbbing of the wound. The irritation, too, came and went in waves, heightening Perken's fever and constraining him to a nightmare struggle to keep his hands off his body; it was as though the minor pain were a decoy, serving the greater agony within him. A soft pattering caught his ear and, looking round, he saw his fingers, frenzied by the insect-bites, drumming feverishly on the woodwork of the cart; till now he had not known that they were moving. Fever was decomposing all his ideas like carrion rotting underground—then a more violent jolt heaved him up to the surface. It seemed to him as if two forces had conspired to swing him back to consciousness—Claude's remark, and a sudden lurch forward of the cart—and he could not distinguish one from the other. He was so weak that all sensations seemed identical, and this unbearable awakening flung him back into a life that he was longing to escape and, in the selfsame

241

moment, back upon himself, the self he wanted to regain. He struggled to fix his thoughts on something, and tried to hoist himself up to see the new fire which had just sprung up, but, before he could move, a mine exploded somewhere far ahead; he heard the clods of earth rain down with a low, muffled roar. The Mois' dogs started barking.

"You know, Claude, the column's all we need bother about and, so long as the railroad isn't finished, we can deal with it all right. All their lines of communication go a long way back; it's up to us to strike at them far in the rear and cut off the vanguard. Then we can secure their guns. It's feasible enough. The great thing is to get there in time. Damn this fever! When I'm through with it, I'd like at least . . . Do you hear me, Claude?"

"Yes, old chap, I'm listening."

"Well, I'd like to feel my death had . . . forced their freedom on them."

"What can that matter to you?"

Perken shut his eyes wearily. Hopeless it was, trying to make another human being understand!

"Is the wound hurting you again?"

"Only at the really bad jolts. But I'm too weak for that to be natural. It'll start again presently."

He looked towards the mountain-tops, then to the hill where the mine had just exploded. To focus the field-glasses, he had to prop himself against the side of the cart, but his head kept swaying from side to side; at last he steadied it.

"I couldn't even fire a shot, in this state!"

On the hillside a string of buffalo-carts was bringing up railway-material; the Siamese cartmen tipped
the sleepers out, one by one, and drove off again,
circling round the last to fall with clockwork regular-
ity—like Grabot circling round his grindstone. The
sleepers dropped without a sound—they might have
been falling in another world—but each impact
thudded in Perken's knee. For it was not only on
his dead hopes the railroad, battering its way ahead
towards the mountains, was to pass, but over his
dead limbs as well, over his decaying eyes and ears
corroded by the earth. He heard the sound not with
his ears but in the pulsing of his arteries—dull thuds
of falling timber; and he knew that, though in his
own country he might have recovered, here he must
die. On the little nucleus of hopes that was his very
life the world would set its stranglehold, clamping
those iron tracks upon it, like a prisoner's chains.
And nothing in the universe could ever compensate
him for his past and present sufferings; to be a living
man was even more absurd than dying! Ever more
numerous, towering high against the molten glare
of noon, pillars of smoke ribbed the skyline with a
gigantic palisade; and in his mind the heat, the
lurching cart, his fever, the baying of the dogs, the
twinges of his wound, the sleepers falling like so
many clods of earth upon his body—all seemed mingling indistinguishably with the barrier of smoke, the
empire of the forest and of death, in an inferno of

abandoned hopes. Beyond the drone of the mosquitoes buzzing in his ears, along the valley from one end to the other, dogs were howling—others, across the hills, replying—and their clamor echoed through the forest to the horizon's edge, filling the interspaces of the smoke with sound. He was a prisoner still, penned in the world of men as in a dungeon, a mad world of smoke-wraiths and lurking perils like dim creatures of the under-earth. And Claude was here beside him, Claude who would go on living, who believed in life as some believe their tortures are human. . . . Claude, too, was hateful now! Alone. He was alone with his fever coursing between his head and knee, alone with the one thing loyal to him yet—his hand, lying upon his thigh.

He had seen his hand thus several times before—as something apart, something quite independent of him. At rest now on his thigh, his hand was gazing calmly up at him. It was his sole companion as he plunged down into a gulf of loneliness, with a smooth feel of tepid water on his skin. When, for a moment, he came up to the surface, he remembered that a man's hands are clenched when the death-agony sets in. . . . Yes, he was positive of that. In his precipitate flight towards a world primeval as the forest, a hateful thought persisted in his mind: that hand of his, that white thing yonder, with its fingers higher than the heavy palm, its nails clawing the threads of the trouser-seam, somehow recalled the spiders hooked to their webs in the warm leafage;

like the spiders dangling in the viscid undergrowth, it hung poised before his fascinated eyes, as he floundered through a world of formless things. And that hand was—death.

Claude looked at him; the wild dogs' baying was strangely congruous with that haggard, unshaven face, those eyelids drooping not with sleep but with approaching death. And this was the one man in the world who had loved him, not for the sake of childish memories, but for his present self and all he meant to be. Claude dared not touch him. But then Perken's head struck against the woodwork of the cart; Claude raised it and propped it with the topee, uncovering his forehead. As Perken opened his eyes the sunlight flooded them, devastating light, yet vibrant with joy. Some branches, bare of insects, glided past between him and the zenith, quivering like the air, like the last Lao girl he had possessed. But now the world of men, even the solid earth drifting past beneath him with its trees and animals, had lost their meaning; he only knew that white immensity, the kingdom of the light, and a tragic inward exultation that little by little overpowered his senses, throbbing with the muffled tremor of his heart.

Now he heard no voice but his own; it seemed that he and he alone could hold communion with the world of fire drawing his soul up from the forest depths; none but he express his wound's response to that sublime effulgence. The words re-echoed in his mind. "It seems to me that I shall stake myself, all

245

that I am, on the moment of my death." Life was
yonder, in the dazzling light that swallowed up the
earth; and, in the fiery throbbing of his veins, the
enemy. Yet they were not at strife; his heart would
stop, and, like the world, be absorbed into the om-
nipotent insistence of the light. He had no hand, no
body now; nothing but pain. What did that word
mean: "failure"? Under the lids his eyes were blades
of searing fire. A mosquito settled on an eyelid; he
could not move. Claude propped his head against a
roll of canvas, and dragged the sun-helmet down
over his eyes. The shadow cast him back upon himself.

He saw himself again tumbling, drunk, into a
river, and singing lustily against the boisterous eddies. Now, too, death compassed him on every side,
like the shimmering air, from horizon to horizon.
Nothing would ever give a meaning to his life—not
even this sudden ecstasy that merged him in the sunlight. Men walked the earth, men who believed in
their passions, their sorrows, their own existence—
insects under the leaves, a teeming multitude beneath the far-flung canopy of death. And the thought
of it thrilled him with an immense joy, joy abound-
ing in his heart, his limbs, joy drumming in his wrists
and temples and pulsing at his heart, pounding out
the rhythm of universal madness streaming up into
the sun. And yet—no man had ever *died;* all had
but drifted into nothingness like the smoke-clouds
yonder dissolving into air, like the forest and the

temples. He, only he, would die, be wrenched out of the scheme of things.

His hand came back to life. It did not move at all, but he could feel the blood-stream throbbing in it, and heard its fluent undertone, timed to the lapping of the river. And, waiting on the threshold of his mind, were memories, ready to pounce, and only kept at bay by the weak menace of his half-clenched fist. Their gradual onset, like the twitching of his fingers, pointed to the end. In his death-agony they would launch their mass-attack, dense as those smoke-clouds drifting towards him with a sound of baying dogs and distant tomtoms. He gritted his teeth, mad with longing to escape his body and merge into the flaming sky that hung above him as above a prey. A stab of intolerable pain, as if a limb were being torn off, shot up his body from his knee. Deep in the bowels of the earth a tunnel loomed before his eyes, a tunnel that was caving in above him. He bit his lip savagely, until it bled.

Claude saw the film of blood upon his teeth; but pain, he realized, was his friend's safeguard against death—suffering, he was still alive. With a sudden swerve of his imagination he saw himself in Perken's place; little as he loved life, never had he clung to it so intensely as at this moment. Blood trickled down Perken's chin in scarlet runlets, like the blood that had trickled from the bullet in the gaur's head; all Claude could do was to stare at the red, gnawing teeth—and wait.

"If I'm remembering things," Perken thought, "that means I'm dying." Like the Stiengs round the hut, all his past life crouched on the threshold of his mind, biding its time relentlessly. "After all, perhaps one doesn't remember. . . ." Yet he kept watch against the past, as on his hand. But, for all his efforts, he could not help recalling how he had flung down his revolver and walked towards the Stiengs across the slanted rays of sunset. But that, surely, was no presage of *his* death; all that had happened to another man, in some previous existence. Once he was back at home the problem would be to get the better somehow of those damned mines pounding upon his fever. Another spasm of pain convulsed him, and he knew that never would he be "back at home"; it was as if he had detected it in the savor of his blood. In his agony he bit deep into his underlip, grinding his teeth upon the bristles of his beard. His mind reeled in an ecstasy of pain; should it grow intenser, surely it would transform him into a madman, into a woman in her birth-pangs screaming for her hour to pass . . . yes, at this moment, new lives were being born into the world, throughout the world. It was not his childhood, as he had expected, that was coming back, but others who had passed away; death summoned up the dead. "Let's hope they don't bury me alive!" But there his hand was, watching, with all his memories behind it, like the eyes of the savages that night, red-glowing in the darkness. No, they would not bury him alive.

"His face has gradually lost all human semblance," Claude thought. Confronted with the vanity of human life, sickened by silence and the irrefutable arraignment of the universe that is the death of one we love, Claude felt his shoulders stiffening with horror, a horror that seemed immutable, eternal as the sky above the dismal baying of dogs, dying away at last into the dazzling silence. Mightier than the forest and the sky, death clutched his head and swung it roughly round to watch the eternal combat between death and life. "How many others," Claude wondered, "at this very hour are watching other deathbeds?" Under the sun of Asia, in the European night, in every corner of the world, men were dying, appalled, they too, by the frustration of their lives, and full of rancor for their fellows who would see another dawn—and nearly all of them were seeking consolation from their gods. Ah, if only they existed, those gods of theirs, and he might, even at the cost of never-ending torment, howl in their faces, like the baying dogs, the bitter truth—that no hope of heaven, no promise of reward, nothing can justify the end of any human life! Could he but circumvent the sheer futility of shouting his resentment at the bright indifference of the sun, the closed eyes of the dying man, those blood-stained teeth gnawing the tattered lips . . . and see no more that tortured face, the spectacle of that immense defeat! Perken's lips began to move.

"There is . . . no death. There's only . . . I

. . . " One finger contracted on his thigh. "I who . . . am dying."

With a rush of hatred Claude recalled a prayer of his childhood. "O Lord, be with us in our last agony. . . ." Ah, could he but express by look or gesture, if not by words, the desperate fraternity that was wrenching him out of himself! He passed his arm round Perken's shoulders.

Perken gazed at him as if he were a stranger, an intruder from another world.

VINTAGE BELLES-LETTRES

A free catalogue of Vintage Books *will be sent at your request. Write to* Vintage Books, 457 Madison Avenue, New York, New York 10022